To Trifecta Publishing House who took a chance on this series.

HER DESERT HORSEMAN

MARIE TUHART

DEAR READER

The country of Bashir is a fictional place. They have their own customs and different rules for titles.

The title of Lady before someone's name is a sign of respect and not an official title.

In book 1 – Once Catherine becomes engaged to Malik she becomes the Crown Princess, once they marry she will become queen.

In all the books, once the heroine is engaged to the hero they will become princess-to-be and when they marry will carry the princess title.

I have taken liberties in creating my own country, it is a progressive country and looking toward the future.

Editor: Elizabeth Jewell

Cover Art by Designed by Diana

Formatted by Monica Corwin

❧ I ❧

Rafi al-Hakim cursed the timing of the information he'd received on Kalif today. He had no choice but to follow up on it before Kalif's men moved to a new camp. He'd pushed his horse Shadow as hard as he dared to get back to the palace in time, but he was still late. His only saving grace was it was Sunday, and no one would be at the stables when he arrived.

With precise care, he brought Shadow onto the palace grounds without alerting any guards. He grinned. His days of sneaking in and out of the palace were good training for what he was doing now.

He quickly rubbed down Shadow and made sure he had fresh food and water before making his way toward the palace. Because he was so late, he didn't have time to change clothes. He was still in his black caftan and headdress. If anyone in his family found out what he was doing, there would be hell to pay, but he had to do something to help the family get rid of the poppy growers.

Footsteps echoed across the courtyard, and Rafi froze, his back to the brick wall in the garden. He kept his breathing slow and even. Waiting. He almost let out a laugh. Here was the fun-loving prince, the one everyone called playful and flirty. A smile crept over his lips; he would continue to let them think like that. It allowed him to do his spying without anyone being the wiser.

The guard passed, and Rafi continued to the side of the palace where the balcony was. He'd used the balcony to sneak in and out of the palace as a kid and through his teenage years; it served him well now.

He quickly climbed one of the big desert willow trees, then made the jump to the balcony, catching himself on the edge before vaulting over. He grunted, taking slightly longer than usual to make the climb. Was he already slowing down at thirty-two? Still plenty of agility in his bag of tricks.

Rafi landed on the balcony with a soft touch, then froze as he saw a woman standing on the balcony looking out at the garden. Damn, there was no way for him to slip away. Then she turned and Rafi was stunned.

Her raven hair flowed around her shoulders, and her eyes were soft and inviting. He couldn't quite tell their color. Blue jeans clung to her thighs, and her colorful blouse flattered her figure.

"Don't be frightened," he said in a tone he reserved for gentling one of his mares.

The woman tilted her head and took a step back. She looked from him to the garden and back to him as if debating what to do.

"Please." Rafi held out his hand. "I won't hurt you. I promise."

She gave a snort. "Sure." She took a step toward the guest bedroom. The bedroom they'd set aside for Zain's new teacher. Wow, who knew Zain's teacher would be this beautiful?

"Who are you?" she asked in a low tone.

Her soft voice drew him in. "No one dangerous." He moved closer to her, watching her. So far she didn't seem like the type who would bolt, but she'd kept her gaze on him as well.

"If you're not dangerous, then why are you dressed all in black with your face covered?" She waved her hand at him.

Rafi had forgotten how he was dressed. "It was necessary." He crept forward one step at a time until he was in front of her. She flinched and raised her hand as if to defend herself. "I would never hit a woman." He reached up and unwound the headdress from around his face. "And who are you, my beautiful lady?" He already knew the answer but wanted to see what she said.

"No one special and certainly not beautiful!" She let out a bitter laugh.

He didn't like the way she said she wasn't special; from where he was standing, she was very special. He captured her hand in his. Her eyes widened with surprise. Rafi hid a smile, lifted her hand to his lips, and kissed her knuckles. "A beautiful woman waiting for her prince to arrive."

"I think you've been out in the sun too long." There was laughter in her voice. "I'm not princess material."

"I beg to differ." He heard voices and glanced toward the garden. The guards were making their rounds, and he didn't want them to notice him. Time to beat a retreat. "Alas, I must go. I promise you, no harm will come to you here in the palace. I am a friend, not a foe."

"But—" she started to protest.

Rafi caught the guards closing in out of the corner of his eyes. He couldn't afford for her to bring attention to them. He leaned down and captured her lips with his. Sweet nectar of the gods invaded his senses. She tasted like honey. When he broke the kiss, he promised himself to kiss her again soon.

He stepped around her and then rapidly made his way down the balcony to his room. Later, he promised himself. Later he'd get to know Zain's schoolteacher better.

Bobbie Anderson let out a breath as she opened the balcony doors and stepped out. She'd arrived in the Middle Eastern country of Bashir two hours ago. She'd been escorted through customs, driven to the palace, and shown to her room. The maid let her know before she left that she would be back at four to escort Bobbie to her meeting with the crown princess.

She let the scents of jasmine, rose, and pure air flow through her. She needed to be outside after being cooped up in a plane for so long. Not that her journey had been that hard.

Yes, the flight from Seattle to London had been long, but she'd been booked into first class and her every whim catered to. The seats even turned into beds, so she couldn't complain she hadn't gotten enough rest. Her layover in London had only been an hour, barely enough time to run to the bathroom and find her next gate.

The flight to Bashir was just a little over two hours, and again she been put into first class. Bobbie had argued with the crown princess over the phone when told of the arrangements, but the crown princess had insisted.

Now she gazed out at the beautiful garden below her, and a sense of contentment filled her. Off in the distance she could see a large wall that encircled the palace grounds. She turned her face up to the sun and let it all soak in.

The warmth sank into her skin. While Seattle did get a lot of rain, the summers were nice. Her discontentment wasn't with the weather, but her life. Had she made the right decision in leaving everything she knew for a country she didn't?

A noise caused her to turn her head to the left. Someone dressed all in black was climbing over the railing. Her hand rose to her throat. Should she yell out at someone? Run back into her room? Before she could make a decision a dark gaze met hers.

"Don't be frightened." His voice was low.

Yeah, right. She took a step back when he moved forward, her eyes darting for an escape.

"Please." He held his hand out. "I won't hurt you. I promise." His voice was low and soothing.

"Sure," she said, stepping toward the bedroom. "Who are you?" Bobbie rolled her eyes. What a question to ask! She should be screaming her head off. But she wasn't. His dark gaze was calm and not wild as she would expect of someone up to no good, and there was his stance. Relaxed and open. He intrigued her.

"No one dangerous." He moved closer.

"If you're not dangerous, then why are you dressed all in black with your face covered?" She gestured to his black robe and head covering. She kept her gaze on him, watching for any fast movements. Bobbie wasn't stupid, plus she'd had self-defense training.

"It was necessary."

He was in front of her now. She flinched as his hand rose, and she prepared to defend herself. His eyes widened. "I would never hit a woman." He unwound the fabric from around his face. His eyes twinkled at her, and his lips tilted up into a half smile. "And who are you, my beautiful lady?"

"No one special and certainly not beautiful!" He had to be kidding. Her skin was quite pale, and it didn't help she had dark hair; she always looked washed out.

"Yes." This time when he moved he captured her hand. Before she could react, he lifted it to his mouth and kissed the back of it. "A beautiful woman waiting for her prince to arrive."

Bobbie laughed; she couldn't help herself. "I think you've been out in the sun too long. I'm not princess material."

"I beg to differ." His gaze turned from her to the garden. "Alas, I must go. I promise you no harm will come to you here in the palace. I am a friend, not a foe."

"But—" Her words were cut off as he leaned forward, brushed a kiss against her lips, then stepped around her.

By the time she commanded her body to turn around he was gone. Her fingers fluttered to her lips. They still tingled from his brief, soft kiss. A giggle escaped her lips. She'd been kissed by a bandit, or at least that's what she was going to call him. Probably one of the palace staff playing a game.

That didn't explain why he was climbing onto the balcony, but that was a puzzle to work out later. Bobbie turned and went back into her room. She had just enough time to unpack, eat a snack, and freshen up before her meeting with the crown princess.

Bobbie pushed down her nerves as the maid led her through the palace to meet with the crown princess. She was going to need a map to get around this place. Luckily, she'd spend most of her time in the classroom with her student, in her room, or out exploring.

The maid knocked on the door, then opened it. "Roberta Anderson, crown princess." The maid gestured for Bobbie to enter, and after she did, left and closed the door.

"Bobbie," Crown Princess Catherine said, and she stood. "I'm so glad you're here." Catherine walked over and took her hand. "Come sit down and we can talk."

Bobbie had told the crown princess to use her nickname when they'd first talked; she didn't like being called Roberta, as it reminded her of what a mess her life had been. "I'm glad to be here, crown princess," Bobbie said as she was led over to the sofa.

"Now, what did I say the last time we talked?"

"Catherine, sorry." Bobbie quelled her nervousness.

"It's fine. The first thing I learned is the royal family is informal in their home. We only do titles and such at formal events." Catherine sat down in the chair next to Bobbie and pushed her reddish-brown hair back. "How was your flight?"

"It was perfect. I thank you again for making it easy for me." Bobbie smiled. Catherine was so open and cheery. Bobbie had noticed it on their calls, but now she could see Catherine almost humming with excitement.

"I'm so happy you accepted the job. I wanted the best and from everything I'd heard about you, you are the best."

"Thank you. I plan to do my best." A knock sounded before the door was opened. A young woman walked in with a tray and set it on the table before leaving.

"Refreshments." Catherine leaned forward. "I wasn't sure what you'd prefer to drink so there's coffee, tea, and juice." She gestured to the two silver pots and glass jug. "Plus there's cheese, fruit, and nuts to nibble on."

"Juice is fine." Bobbie was surprised at the wide selection, but then she remembered everything in her room. "I had a light snack in my room before coming down."

"Good. Is your room satisfactory?" Catherine asked as she poured juice into a glass for Bobbie, handed it to her, and then poured herself a cup of tea.

"Oh, yes." Bobbie took a sip of the juice. The mango flavor burst on her taste buds. "It's a beautiful room. I didn't expect it to be so large."

Catherine smiled. "We want you to be comfortable."

"I am." Bobbie sat her glass down. "Do you and the king still have concerns about Zain?"

Catherine let out a sigh. "Yes. I told you about how he'd been hurt, and now that he's out of the hospital, we want him to feel at home. But he's missed a lot of schooling."

"You said Zain was seven." Bobbie mentally reviewed everything she'd been told.

"Yes. We only found out recently he's missed a lot of his school time. Plus ... " Catherine closed her eyes, and her teacup shook in her hand.

"What is it?" Bobbie didn't like how Catherine was reacting. Yes, Bobbie had had training as a special needs teacher; it was one of the reasons she had been recommended for this job.

"Zain still won't speak." Catherine set her cup down. "We had hoped after his hands healed, he'd come out of his shell."

"Doesn't he speak at all?" She knew of the trauma the little boy had suffered because of his father.

"He'll whisper to me or Malik but no one else." Catherine's eyes filled with tears.

"It may take time, Catherine." How could she explain that some children never fully healed? Bobbie's heart grew heavy; she didn't want to dash Catherine's hope. "From what you've told me, Zain has had a pretty hard life."

"Yes." Catherine sniffled and brushed a tear away. "We've found out more. Since his father's death, people are more willing to speak up."

"Have you had any thoughts about putting Zain into public school? My understanding is you are working on upgrading your school system."

A smile curved Catherine's lips. "Yes, we are." They talked about Catherine's plans to improve the country's school system so the children had more choices in education, but also how they wanted to build a university in

Bashir to allow their people to get their degrees and continue to work in the country.

"Those are big plans." Bobbie was fascinated. Her degrees in primary schooling and special needs kept her busy, and she loved the idea of allowing the younger children to pursue what they wanted in school.

She'd found too many times that parents would push children in the direction they wanted, not what the children wanted. Allowing kids to explore different subjects and be exposed to different cultures was excellent.

"They are." Catherine looked down at her watch. "Oh, my goodness, we've been talking for hours. Dinner is in thirty minutes, and I need to get changed."

"I understand." Bobbie stood up. The time had passed quickly.

"We meet in the family room at seven for drinks, and then dinner."

"Oh, but—" Bobbie's hands fluttered in front of her.

"No buts. You are a member of the household."

"What do I wear?" Bobbie ran through her meager clothing options.

"Oh, dear." Catherine smiled. "I didn't mean to alarm you. Wear whatever you're comfortable in, I just ask no jeans. At dinner you can meet the rest of the family."

"Sure." Bobbie swallowed her nerves. She hadn't expected this.

"Don't worry, no one bites." Catherine led her out of the room, and Bobbie's stomach turned over. Dinner with the royal family? She wasn't prepared for being part of the royal family.

Bobbie smoothed her hand over the long skirt she wore as the maid showed her to the family room. She hadn't realized there was a public section of the palace and a private section until Catherine had pointed it out earlier.

While Bobbie changed she ran through all she knew about Bashir's royal family. King Malik had recently become king after his father had had a heart attack. Malik had three brothers; none were married yet.

Catherine's wedding was due to take place in a month, and now that she thought about it, Bobbie realized how calm Catherine was about it.

"Here we are, ma'am," the maid said.

"Thank you." Bobbie took a deep breath and walked through the open double doors. Catherine and Malik stood by the bar area, with another man behind the bar pouring drinks.

The room had dark wood paneling, but the sheer curtains on the windows let a lot of light in, making the room bright. Sofas and chairs were placed around the room with a colorful rug on the hardwood floor.

"Bobbie." Catherine motioned her over.

"Catherine. King Malik." Bobbie gave a slight bow.

"Malik." He grinned, taking her hand and shaking it. "No formalities."

Bobbie nodded her head.

"Drink?" the man behind the bar asked.

"A club soda, please." She barely kept herself from exclaiming over his gorgeous bright blue eyes.

"Hassan, this is Zain's teacher, Bobbie," Catherine said as Hassan handed Bobbie her drink.

"It's a pleasure to meet you, Bobbie." Hassan's gaze swept over her from head to toe. "You look nothing like any teacher I've met before."

"Oh, stop flirting," a female voice said.

Bobbie, flustered by Hassan's attention, turned to see a woman with blonde hair and a grin on her face walking across the room. "Hi, I'm Sara. Welcome to Bashir." She looked at the man behind the bar. "And ignore Hassan."

"I wasn't flirting, just stating a fact." He reached over the bar, snagged Sara's hand, and brought it to his lips. "Besides, you're the only woman I have eyes for."

Bobbie's heart swelled at the love for Sara she saw in this man's eyes.

"You'll have to excuse them, they've only been engaged two months," Catherine said.

"Hey, I never complained when you two made moon eyes at each other," Hassan said.

"Moon eyes?" Malik burst out laughing.

"Hassan is right." Another male voice added as he

strode into the room and up to them. "I am Khalid, the fourth brother in this crazy family."

"Hi." Bobbie took his outstretched hand and shook it.

"Khalid is in charge of security, so you'll be talking with him about everything," Malik said.

"Oh." Bobbie's mind wandered back to the man on the balcony today. Should she tell Khalid? No, she decided. There was something about her balcony man, an instinct she couldn't quite explain to herself that told her he wasn't dangerous. She wasn't ready to expose him to palace security; not yet, anyway.

"There are security protocols I must ask you to keep," Khalid said.

"Nothing too onerous, right?" Catherine said, leaning toward him with a smile.

"I promise, Catherine. Nothing out of the ordinary." Khalid smiled at Catherine. They had a rapport, which was reassuring to Bobbie. So far there was an ease here among the family members. What would happen if she announced a prowler lurked on the grounds? Her belly knotted with guilt as this announcement died on her lips.

"And where is Rafi?" Malik asked.

"Right here."

Bobbie looked up when she heard the voice. That deep, sensual voice was one she'd heard before, earlier this afternoon. Her eyes widened as she took in the man standing just inside the door in a pair of black slacks and black shirt. The man she couldn't stop thinking about. He was her bandit from earlier today. A brother. His self-confidence, even arrogance, when she'd caught him suddenly made sense. He must have his reasons for his escapades. Gratitude that she hadn't revealed his furtive activities melted the tension gripping her body even as curiosity bloomed.

R afi tried to keep from staring at the woman standing with his family. The beautiful woman from the balcony. He kept reliving the taste of her lips. Would she keep her silence about him? Or blow his cover, destroying his chance to find out Kalif's location? Not that he didn't trust his brothers, but being an effective spy meant the fewer people who knew of his pursuits, the better.

"Rafi, this is Bobbie, Zain's teacher," Malik said.

"You're Zain's teacher?" He kept his voice neutral so as not to give away his knowledge.

"Yes." Her eyes narrowed.

"My apologies." He crossed the room and grasped her hand before lifting it to his lips and kissing the back of it.

Vanilla and rose scents tickled his nose. "You are much too young and beautiful."

Color rose to her cheeks, and Rafi found himself fascinated by Bobbie. Bobbie, what an unusual name.

"Rafi is the family flirt," Hassan said.

"Guilty." Rafi kept her hand in his, enjoying the feel of her skin against his. "I also take care of the horses." And he wanted to take care of her. Whoa, he reined in his thoughts. They barely knew each other, but his dominant side was wide awake and focused on her.

Her hazel eyes grew bright. "Horses? You have a stable here?"

"Yes, we do." Rafi grinned. "Maybe after dinner I can show them to you."

Malik let out a laugh. "That's almost as bad as saying let me show you my etchings."

Rafi glared at his brother, then returned his gaze to Bobbie. "Bobbie, is that a nickname?"

"Yes." Her voice was soft and quiet.

"And?" he prompted.

"Roberta," she whispered. "But I prefer Bobbie." Her chin came up. "So what kind of horses do you have?"

Just then the doors were opened to the dining room. "I'll tell you over dinner." Slipping her arm through his, he guided her in for the meal. Life around the palace had just become more interesting.

Two hours later, Rafi sat at the dinner table totally relaxed for once. He'd talked with Bobbie about the horses he raised. Her attention never wavered. Another horse lover, what fun they would have together. After a bit, the conversation turned to Malik and Catherine's upcoming wedding.

Their family was growing. The new wing was almost finished and that would help with space. Also his parents were spending more and more time at the summer palace in the south, easing the pressure on the main palace. The only thorn on the rose bush, so to speak, was Kalif.

In the two months since Sara had been hurt, they'd searched and searched for Kalif with no luck. Even Rafi on his secret missions hadn't been able to find out where Kalif was hiding.

But he'd been able to get information to help Khalid find more of the poppy fields, freeing their people and ridding themselves of the poppy, at least for the moment.

"Any news on Kalif?" Malik asked, bringing Rafi's thoughts back to the present.

"No." Khalid sighed. "We've raided two more poppy fields that have cropped up."

"Poppies? Aren't they just flowers?" Bobbie asked.

"I wish," Sara muttered. "Poppies can be smoked; technically, they're the source of opium."

"And many of our older generation have become addicted to smoking opium," Hassan said. "We're working to eradicate it, but it takes time."

Bobbie nodded. "Drugs are like any other addiction, hard to get over."

There was a wistful tone in her voice.

"Bobbie," Rafi said. "Tell us about your childhood." The second he said the words, her face closed down and her eyes grew dim.

"Not much to tell." She shrugged her shoulders.

Rafi glanced across the table at Catherine, who shook her head. "Well, then, shall we tell you about ours?"

"I'm a little tired," Bobbie said, placing her napkin on the table. "If you would excuse me, I'm going to go to my room." She pushed back her chair.

Rafi rose with her. Damn it, he didn't mean to scare her away.

"I'm fine," she said. "I can find my way back to my room. Please forgive my abruptness. I have a headache starting. I would like nothing more than to hear about your family another time. Thank you for your hospitality. Good night." She turned and left the room.

"Good going, brother," Khalid muttered.

"What?" Rafi retook his seat.

"Scared her off. I wanted to learn more about her," Khalid said.

"As if you don't already know." Rafi was well aware anyone coming into the royal household was well investigated.

"I want more than just cold facts. She's a beautiful woman," Khalid said.

"And not for you." Rafi pinned his brother with a hard

stare. "Stay away from her." With that he stood and left the room.

Within a minute, Rafi realized he was acting out of character even for him. His dominance was showing, but there was something about Bobbie that got under his skin. Their meeting on the balcony earlier today had been electric for him. He had been instantly attracted to her. Something that hadn't happened in a while. And he wanted to explore things with her.

Rafi made his way out into the garden. Maybe a stroll around would distract him from Bobbie and allow him to make plans for his next meeting with his informant.

Bobbie wandered around the garden. Her proclamation she could find her way back to her room had been a mistake. She'd take a wrong turn and instead found a door to the garden.

This was much better than going back to her room, however. Here she was in the fresh air and could remain calm, rather than be cooped up in her room. When Rafi had asked about her childhood, she'd frozen. Bobbie let out a sigh. One of these days she'd get over her not-so-stellar childhood, but it didn't look like today would be it. Hopefully she hadn't offended her hosts during her first family dinner. She was already struggling with how formal to be. She was encouraged to be casual, but she was an employee. It was awkward finding the middle ground, and then, on top of that, to lose her cool when the perfectly natural topic of her childhood arose. Her usual answers to such questions had abandoned her when she needed them most.

Spying the gazebo, she climbed the white wooden steps and took a seat. The smell of jasmine and rose filled her senses. But her mind was in turmoil.

Her mother hadn't been a loving woman, but Bobbie's dad had more than made up for it until he passed away when she was sixteen. Her life had fallen apart. Her mother had blamed Bobbie for her father's death.

God, her mother's image rose in her mind. Her eyes had been red from crying and her voice hoarse as she yelled at Bobbie. Bobbie took a stuttering breath as she recalled the venom in her mother's voice when she'd yelled, "If it wasn't for you wanting to become a vet, your father wouldn't have gambled to get the money to send you to school."

The impact of her mother's statement caused her stomach to clench even now. She hadn't known they were that strapped for money, or that her father had kept gambling even when he'd lost.

Neighbors and friends had tried to tell Bobbie her mother was just speaking out in grief and she didn't mean it, but Bobbie knew she did. Her mother had resented Bobbie for sharing his love of horses.

A bitter little laugh escaped her lips. For the next three

years she'd endured her mother's barbs, kept her nose clean, and worked her butt off in school. She'd even gotten a part-time job. The day she'd turned eighteen, she'd come home from her shift at the local fast food place to see all her belongings on the porch of the house. Her mother had stood beside them, arms folded, and told her she was eighteen, time to get out.

Bobbie closed her eyes as a sharp pain punched her in the stomach. Her mother hadn't cared where her daughter had gone or what she'd done. Bobbie had gathered her belongings, loaded them into her old car, and left. Luckily, she'd been paid that day, so she had enough to find herself a cheap hotel room.

A noise had her turning her head. Rafi stood at the entrance of the gazebo.

"I'm sorry," he said.

"For what?" His presence pulled her out of her thoughts, and it was a good thing. She really didn't want to dwell on the past.

"Disturbing your peace. I'll leave." He turned.

"Please don't." The words rushed from her mouth. She really didn't want to be alone with her thoughts. "Stay."

His grin lit up his face. "I thought you were going to your room." He crossed over to her and took a seat on the bench.

"I got lost," she said, then laughed. "I'm going to need a map."

"You'll catch on fast."

They fell silent and only the sounds of insects filled the gazebo. Bobbie studied Rafi from the corner of her eye. He was a handsome man, but it was more than that. She just couldn't put her finger on it. Her body reacted to his, and her lips tingled from that brief kiss this afternoon on the balcony.

"Why were you climbing the balcony railing today if you're a member of the family?" she asked.

"Ah, that." His eyes twinkled. "Can we keep it between us, please?"

Bobbie frowned. "I don't like keeping secrets."

"I promise I have a really good reason." He lifted his hand and ran a finger over her cheek. "I'll tell my family in time, just not now."

"Why do I suspect you're up to no good?"

"I promise, I'm not." He shifted closer and Bobbie sighed.

"For now, but ... " His finger traced her lips, stopping her words. Heat filled her from his touch.

"I'll tell them soon." He trailed his finger from her lips down her neck, causing her to arch.

His touch was feathery soft and sent shivers of awareness through her veins. Her breath caught in her throat as he traced the opening of her blouse.

"Rafi." His name slipped from her lips.

"Beautiful Bobbie," he whispered, his warm breath brushing her skin.

"I'm not," she denied.

"You are." His hand slid behind her neck under her dark hair.

"Why are you flirting with me?" Bobbie had no expectations where her looks were concerned. She was pretty ordinary.

"Because I want to. Because that kiss we shared is all I can think about."

He watched her with those dark eyes of his. This close she could see little speckles of blue in his eyes, but not the solid blue like Hassan's.

"Why did you kiss me on the balcony?" Her hand covered her mouth. Now why had she asked him that? Maybe because she wanted to make sure she wasn't just some conquest or challenge for him?

His eyes brightened and his fingers tightened on her neck. "Because I wanted to. Like I do now." He dropped his head and brushed his lips over hers.

Bobbie's heart skipped a beat when their lips touched. Why was she allowing him to do this? She barely knew him. But she couldn't seem to help herself. Her willpower flew away when his lips touched to hers. A longing inside her swelled.

He only brushed her lips once again before kissing her cheek and then sitting back. He kept his hand on her neck, but instead of making her feel restrained, the touch made her feel cherished. A shiver went up her spine. No man had affected her like this, not even when she had played in the BDSM community in Seattle.

Rafi kept his gaze on her, and she was drowning in his eyes, but there was more. Something shifted inside her. She could barely breathe. It wasn't out of fear, but a desire she'd never felt. A need building inside her.

This was crazy. She had just met him. She didn't fall in lust with men. Never had. Yes, she'd read about it in romance novels, but that was fantasy. His gaze was so intense, and another thought occurred to her. Was Rafi a dominant?

She had started to lean toward him, and the thought brought her up short. Why would she think that? Yes, he had that air of command around him, but ... what? Yes, he had that dominant male vibe, but it was more; he didn't have to show his domination like other men had, his was natural.

"Your eyes have gone wide and your breathing is shallow. What are you thinking?" he asked.

Heat filled her cheeks. There was no way she could tell him what she was thinking. Kink was private to her.

"Must be something interesting for you to blush like that." A grin played around his lips.

"Rafi, let me go," she whispered.

"Of course." His hand slipped from her neck, and she missed his touch.

Oh, get over it, Bobbie. You don't know this man;

don't make a fool out of yourself. "I really should go to my room." She stood.

"You're running."

Bobbie froze in her tracks. "What makes you say that?"

A sexy smile overtook his lips. "Because you're afraid."

She couldn't deny his words, but he didn't have to know that. "Goodnight, Rafi." She walked out of the gazebo and back to the palace. She would have to watch her step around him, because this man was dangerous to her as a woman. A bit too hard to resist, and her role here did not include being the lover of one of the brothers.

Early the next morning, Catherine showed Bobbie to the room that would serve as a classroom. "You know I don't really expect you to work on your full first day with us," Catherine said as she pushed open the door. The room was large. A lone table and chair sat in the room. "I'm sorry the room is so empty. I wasn't sure what you would need."

Bobbie set her computer bag on the table, then opened it and pulled out a pad of paper and a pen. "I can start working on a list. I do have some supplies coming, but I want to make the room welcoming for Zain."

"The marketplace should have most of what you need; if not, we can order it and have it delivered," Catherine said.

"That's doable; let me get started on a list, and I'll find you when I'm ready to go shopping," Bobbie said.

"I have an event later today," Catherine said with a slight smile. "But I'll find someone to escort you. Just let me know when you're ready." Catherine left the room with a wave, and Bobbie sat down to work.

Several hours later, Bobbie glanced at the list in front of her. She wanted Zain to be comfortable here. The supplies she had coming were more for teaching than decorating. Tapping the pen against her cheek, she glanced up to see Rafi lounging in the doorway.

Her heart sped up. Damn it, why did he affect her this way? Yes, he was a handsome man. Okay, sexy and handsome. But she was here to work, not flirt with one of the princes. She was here to do a job.

"Hi, Rafi," she said, not liking how breathless her voice was.

"Bobbie." The man grinned at her as if he knew how he affected her. He pushed away from the door frame and sauntered into the room. "Catherine sent me to escort you to the marketplace. Are you ready?"

"Catherine sent *you*?" His eyebrows rose at her question, and she ducked her head. "I'm sorry. I didn't mean it the way it came out. I was just surprised." Bobbie hadn't meant to question him like that. Catherine had seen what a flirt he was. What was she playing at? Hopefully she didn't see how Rafi awoke a side of her she'd buried over the years. She really didn't have time for a man in her life.

Too many of them had disappointed her, even in the kink community.

"I had some free time today, and Catherine indicated you wanted to go to the marketplace to pick up some things. I don't mind escorting you."

His dark eyes twinkled with mischief. Bobbie couldn't help the grin that came over her lips. "Fine." She glanced down at her list. "This might take us a while. I have a lot I need to get."

He strode to her desk. His heat called out to her as he stood next to her. "That's one long list," he said as he glanced down at the paper in front of her.

"It is. I want Zain to be comfortable here. I want him to learn and feel safe."

"We all want that. I'll meet you at the front door in fifteen minutes. Does that give you enough time to get ready?"

"I'm ready now." Bobbie picked up her list, folded it, and slid it into the pocket of her jeans. She looked at Rafi. "Am I breaking some rule by going out in jeans?"

"No. I wasn't sure if you needed to go grab your purse or anything else."

"Oh, my goodness, I didn't think about that. I didn't talk to Catherine about how we would pay for the supplies." Bobbie mentally calculated how much credit she had left on her credit card. Not that she led an extravagant lifestyle, but her teacher salary only covered so much.

The feel of his finger against her cheek brought her

out of her musings. She fought not to lean into his touch. Her reaction to Rafi scared her in more than one way. She hadn't been with a man in a year, choosing instead to concentrate on her career.

"There's nothing to worry about. The family will pick up the cost of anything you need. We want Zain to be happy in the classroom as well." Rafi tilted his head. "And we want you to be happy."

Bobbie couldn't stop the shiver of acceptance that went up her spine. They wanted her to be happy? How long had it been since somebody was concerned about her happiness? It'd probably been more than ten years since anyone cared about her happiness. Since her father died.

Her vision turned blurry, and Bobbie blinked quickly to push back the tears filling her eyes. "That's so sweet of you to say," she said softly.

Rafi stared down at her, his dark eyes filled with concern and something else. There was heat there, desire. Bobbie pulled herself together and took a step back, forcing him to drop his hand. "We should probably get moving."

Rafi shook his head and then cupped her elbow to escort her from the room. "Yes, let's get this done, but I want you to know something." He stopped before they crossed the threshold out of the classroom. "You intrigue me and unless you tell me no, I plan on spending time with you. Getting to know you and," he leaned down, "if you allow it, for us to have a relationship."

Every nerve inside her body sprang alive, even as a cold chill swept through her. "We only met yesterday."

"True. But we al-Hakim men know what we want the minute we see it. Just ask Catherine or Sara."

His tone was serious, and Bobbie made a mental note that she needed to talk with either Catherine or Sara because she wasn't sure she could handle a man like Rafi. "Understood. But for today, let's just go shopping."

Rafi grinned. "Shopping it is."

Rafi escorted Bobbie to the front of the palace where they could get to his car. This woman threw him off balance. He thought for sure she was going to tell him no, that she didn't want a relationship with him, but then she surprised him by not saying no; her only objection was they'd only met yesterday.

Her words made him happy because he wanted to pursue a relationship with her. Their brief kisses told him they were compatible. But Bobbie didn't seem to understand just how attracted he was to her, or maybe she did. Something told him she wasn't used to male attention, and he had to wonder if the men she'd been around were blind.

Plus there was the way she'd reacted to a couple of his dominant actions. The hold on the back of her neck—she didn't try to squirm away; instead, she'd held still. And the way her breathing increased in his presence.

Her long dark hair was pulled back into a ponytail this morning, and her hazel eyes sparkled with excitement. He knew most women liked to shop, but he had his suspicions that it was so much more for Bobbie. The excitement came from being able to create a learning space. A space where Zain could feel safe, learn, and be happy.

Hamaz, his bodyguard, stood by the front door. Rafi introduced them and said to Bobbie, "Hamaz is my bodyguard. While you are here, if you need to leave the palace grounds, tell him and he will go with you if I'm not available."

Bobbie's eyes widened. "No one mentioned a bodyguard."

"It's only for when you're outside the palace grounds."

"I will be unobtrusive, Lady Bobbie," Hamaz said.

Rafi turned his gaze to his bodyguard. Lady? While it was a term of respect in his country, it still surprised him. Both Malik's and Hassan's bodyguards had called Catherine and Sara 'lady' before anyone else, and look what had happened there.

"Bashir is a safe country, but since you are connected to the royal family, we take your protection seriously," Rafi said.

"Understood." Bobbie inclined her head. "Unless it's a planned field trip for Zain, I doubt I'll be off the palace grounds very much."

Rafi nodded. Hamaz opened the front door and they walked out. A dark blue SUV sat waiting for them. Rafi helped Bobbie inside the SUV before climbing in beside her. Hamaz climbed into the front passenger seat. Once they were all settled, the driver started the engine and off they went.

"Tell me more about Bashir," Bobbie said after they drove out the palace gates.

"Bashir is a small country. Bashir City is our capital. We are pretty much a self-sustaining country. We grow our own fruits and vegetables, and raise cows and sheep plus wheat and cotton."

"That is so wonderful. How does the poppy growing fall into all this?"

Rafi rubbed his chin. "Our ancestors were not very good at keeping the poppy growing under control. My father tried, but there were so many things that needed fixing in our country." He reached over and took her hand in his. Rafi enjoyed the softness of her skin against his. "My grandfather, when he was king, let the country deteriorate."

"Why would he do that?"

"I suspect my grandfather was addicted to smoking opium like so many other older people in our country, but my father would never say."

"How old were you when your grandfather died?"

"I hadn't been born yet." Rafi found himself wanting to tell her about his family and their country's history, something he hadn't wanted to do with other women in his life.

"I'm sorry." Her fingers closed over his.

"It's okay. When my father became king he found out just how far my grandfather had let things go. So dad concentrated on rebuilding our country and trying to make things better for the people."

"That was a very noble thing for him to do."

"Yes, but thirty-three years later, while our country has rebuilt itself, the poppy growers have been allowed to flourish. I don't blame my father; he had his hands full. But now we have to clean it up."

"Drug addiction is a horrible thing."

"Hassan opened the new drug rehabilitation wing at the hospital, so we're tackling this problem on multiple levels. Getting people the help they need and eradicating the poppy fields."

The car turned, and Bobbie let out a little gasp at what she saw. Rafi smiled. "We've made it to Bashir City proper. The car will have to park a little ways from the market-place. I hope you don't mind walking."

"No, I don't mind. The city is, how do I want to say this, a mixture of old and new. I can see the history but I can also see progress."

Rafi studied Bobbie's face. "You are a very intuitive woman."

"I love history, and I suspect Bashir has a lot of history."

"It does, and I think you'll have fun exploring the marketplace today." The vehicle stopped. Rafi undid his seatbelt and then opened the door and got out. He held his hand out for Bobbie and was pleased when she slipped her hand in his and allowed him to help her out of the vehicle.

Keeping her hand in his, he led her toward the marketplace, with Hamaz following. Rafi kept Bobbie close to his side not only for protection but because he wanted her there.

They turned the corner and Bobbie stopped. "Welcome to the marketplace," Rafi said.

Bobbie's breath caught in her throat. The marketplace was a pleasant surprise. She was expecting just a few shops, but instead there were lots of storefronts with colorful awnings and tents set up with vendors. The smell of incense tickled her nose, and the voices of the people selling and buying mingled in the warm air. "This is fantastic."

"We love the marketplace. It's for everyone and anyone. The storefronts are for more permanent businesses. There are people who come from other regions to sell their wares."

"It's very beautiful." And it was. Bobbie had gone with her father on many occasions to a local flea market. They had so much fun just walking around and seeing everything. The marketplace reminded her of a better time, a happier time in her life.

"Since I just glanced at your list, you need to tell me what's on it so I can get us into the right shops."

Bobbie fished her list from her pocket. "Well, the first thing I'm going to need is some place where we can buy some tables and chairs unless there are some in the palace I can use. I'll need another store where I can pick up some colorful pillows. I also need a throw rug. And then somewhere where I can buy—I hate to call them school supplies, because it's so much more than that."

Rafi pulled the list from her fingers and read it. "This is a long list but I think we have everything here. Catherine said to let you buy whatever you felt was needed. Let's get started."

In the first store Rafi took her to, Bobbie ran her hand over the smooth wood table. The craftsmanship was absolutely wonderful. "Rafi, I need six tables this size. Can we get that?"

"I see no reason why not." Rafi raised his hand and instantly a small man came running.

"Yes, Your Highness. What can I do for you?" the man asked.

Bobbie was startled by the 'Your Highness' from the shopkeeper. She had totally forgotten he was royalty. This man was so down-to-earth he never put on airs, never demanded attention. Although he got lots of attention; she'd noticed that as they'd walked to the shop.

People would stop and look at him, but most didn't approach, as if they knew he was a man on a mission. A couple of vendors called out, and Rafi would raise his hand in acknowledgment as they continued to walk.

"Tamir, this is Bobbie. She is going to be Zain's teacher, and we need to furnish a classroom for him. She's wondering if we can get six of these tables?"

"I am pleased to meet you, Lady Bobbie. How soon do you need the tables?"

Bobbie thought for a moment. She wanted to spend some time with Zain before they started a regular classroom arrangement. "If I could get two tables right away and then the other four in a week, that would be perfect."

"I should be able to do that. I have three of these tables available right now, and getting another three built in a week should not be a problem."

Bobbie looked at the table and then back at Tamir. "You mean these are handcrafted?"

"Of course, my lady. My sons and I craft each and every piece of furniture. We are very proud of our work and our heritage."

"I meant no disrespect, Tamir. It's just that where I'm from things are manufactured. Your furniture is beautiful, and I am humbled that you would make such wonderful tables for me."

Rafi watched the exchange between Tamir and Bobbie. At first he was worried Tamir might be upset by

Bobbie's words, but then she explained and Tamir's face lit up at her compliment.

"What else do you need, my lady?" Tamir asked.

"I will need a couple of chairs. Four at the most."

"I can do that. Follow me and I'll show you what we have, and you can make a decision."

Bobbie looked at Rafi and he smiled. "Go ahead and pick out what you need." Bobbie nodded and followed Tamir. Rafi wandered back to the entrance of the store. "Hamaz, I think you should call the palace and warn them that a delivery truck is going to be coming to the palace. I suspect by the time Bobbie is done we'll need one."

An hour later Rafi and Bobbie made their way out of the shop and down the street. "Why do Hamaz and others call me Lady Bobbie?" she asked.

"It's a sign of respect in our country."

"That's very interesting."

Rafi guided Bobbie to their next stop. He was pretty sure she would be able to find the rest of what she needed for the classroom at this shop. The Bashir Mercantile, as the owner, Jack, liked to call it, had anything and everything.

"Rafi," a booming male voice called out.

Bobbie backed up a step as a large man came striding across the floor.

"It's okay, it's just Jack." Rafi held his hand out. "Jack, good to see you. This is Bobbie. She is Zain's teacher and here to get supplies for her classroom. I figured you'll have everything she needs."

"Well, hello, there, pretty lady."

"If I've got my accent right, you're Australian," Bobbie said.

"You've got a good ear there, and yes, I am Australian. Tell me, what do you need to fill your classroom?"

Bobbie fished her list out of her pocket and handed it to Jack, who looked it over. "What I don't have I can order and have it here within a few days." Jack reached over and took Bobbie's hand. "Let's do some shopping."

Three hours later, Bobbie sank down onto the wicker chair in the outside seating area of the café Rafi had brought her to. Shopping with Jack had been an experience. "Can you explain how Jack came to be in Bashir?" She was still coming to terms with the fact that this Australian Bushman was in the desert country.

Rafi gave a laugh. "Jack came here about five years ago. He liked the city and decided to open his store. We were just rebuilding the marketplace and thought it was a good idea."

"He's very friendly."

"Yes. But then you are special, so he was going to make sure you got everything you needed."

Bobbie ducked her head. "There's nothing special about me."

Rafi reached over and took her hand in his. "I think you're very special, and I don't want you to forget that."

Just then Yusef bustled up with water and a plate of fruit. "Prince Rafi, I'm very honored to have you here today."

"Thank you, Yusef," Rafi said. "Bobbie, would you like something other than water to drink?"

"I'd love some iced tea if you could," Bobbie said.

"Of course, Lady Bobbie. I will also bring out some loukoumades and kahk. Would you like anything else?"

"I think that will be fine," Rafi said. "Thank you, Yusef."

Yusef bowed and bustled off.

"I've noticed that a lot today," Bobbie said.

"What is that?" Rafi took a sip of his water while keeping his gaze on her.

"The slight bow that the shopkeepers give you. Heck, even Jack."

Rafi shook his head. "Jack does it just to annoy me. Everyone else, well, we haven't been able to break them of it. My grandfather was big on protocol. But I think you've noticed that I and my brothers are not. You'll even see it when you meet my parents."

"I actually think it's great that you're all down-to-earth."

"I forget. With Catherine and Sara being from Britain they're used to their royal family, but you're from the US."

"I might be from the US, but I'm well aware of the royal family in England. I just assumed all royal families were like that. But I will admit the first time I talked to Catherine I was really taken aback."

"Yes, Catherine has a way of putting people at ease. Which reminds me, I should take you to the hospital so you're able to see her mural. It's a very nice piece."

"I would like that, but I'm not sure when I'll have time. It's going to take me a couple of days to get the classroom ready, and then I want to spend some time with Zain before I actually start teaching him."

"Why don't I help you get the classroom ready?"

"What?" Bobbie had had enough trouble today ignoring the way her pulse raced with Rafi near. If she spent days with him in the classroom ... she had no idea of what could happen.

"I can go down to the stables early in the morning to take care of what needs to be done and then help you in the classroom. There's no reason you need to do this alone."

"But don't you have other things to do?" She waved her hands in the air. "More princely things?"

"Princely things?" His chest rumbled with laughter.

Bobbie frowned at him, then smiled and laughed. "I couldn't come up with a better word."

Yusef walked back up to their table carrying a pitcher and two glasses filled with ice. Behind him was a waiter with another tray.

"Here you are, iced tea." Yusef sat the glasses on the table, then poured the tea before setting the pitcher down.

He turned to the waiter. "Loukoumades and kahk—if you need anything else, please don't hesitate to ask." The two scurried off.

"These look delicious."

"Yusef makes these fresh every day." Rafi picked up the small plates Yusef had left and put a couple loukoumades on it, along with some fruit, then placed it in front of Bobbie. "They are a fried pastry. Try it."

Bobbie lifted the triangle to her lips and took a bite. Almonds and sugar burst on her tongue. "Oh, my goodness," she said after she swallowed. "It's light and full of flavor."

Rafi nodded as he filled his plate and put two more loukoumades on hers. Bobbie glanced down at them. "I really should eat more fruit," she said.

"Why?" Rafi tilted his head.

"Because it's better for me," she said, eating a piece of watermelon.

"And that's the only reason?"

Bobbie stared at him. "Pretty much. I try to eat as healthy as possible. But I'll admit I do have a sweet tooth." She picked up another piece of the almond pastry and ate it.

"I have a sweet tooth as well." He leaned over to her. "And your kisses will only partly satisfy it."

"Only partly?" The words slipped out before she could prevent them.

Rafi grinned. "When we're in private, I'll—"

"Prince Rafi," a male voice yelled, and then flashes went off.

"Your Highness, new girlfriend?" yelled another male voice.

The flashes and yelling startled Bobbie, so she jumped out of her chair and ran inside the café.

Rafi pasted on a smile, even though he wanted to go after Bobbie. Damn paparazzi.

"Shoo," Yusef yelled, waving his arm at the photographers as several of the employees began pushing them away from the outdoor seating area. "I'm sorry, Prince Rafi. We didn't notice them until it was too late."

"It's quite all right. Did you see where Bobbie went?"

"I believe she fled into the ladies' room. Shall I box this up for you?" Yusef asked.

"Yes, please." Rafi made his way inside. Hamaz tilted his head toward the bathrooms, and Rafi nodded. "Bobbie." He knocked on the door.

"Be out in a minute." Her muffled voice came through the door.

Rafi paced. Usually he didn't mind the press, but he hadn't thought about them butting in on him and Bobbie so soon. He should have. They'd done it to Catherine and Malik, and to Sara and Hassan. When the door opened, he stopped pacing.

Bobbie's face was pale, but she seemed calm.

"I'm sorry." He moved to her side and took her hand in his. "I didn't think they would bother us."

"It's not your fault, but I'd like to go back to the palace now." Her voice was soft.

"Of course." The drive back was made in silence, and Rafi wasn't sure how to breach it. He couldn't blame Bobbie, but he wanted her to talk to him.

"I'm a little tired, so I'm going to go up to my room and rest for a bit." She took two steps, then stopped and turned back to him. "Thank you for taking me shopping and to the café." She kissed him on the cheek, and then she ran up the stairs.

"Trouble?" Catherine asked as she walked into the entryway.

"Paparazzi," he muttered.

"Vultures. Is Bobbie okay?"

Rafi knew how much Catherine hated the press. "I think so. They startled her a bit, but she seems to be okay."

"All right. If you need me, I'll be in Malik's office. We have to go over the last-minute wedding stuff." Catherine gave him a kiss on the cheek before walking toward Malik's office.

Rafi's shoulders relaxed. He'd let Bobbie rest, for now. If she wasn't at dinner tonight that would be another matter altogether. Hamaz stood with the box from Yusef. "Hamaz, if you would make sure a plate is taken to Bobbie's room for her to enjoy later, I'm going down to the stables for a while."

"Very well, Prince Rafi."

B obbie sat down in the only chair in the classroom and lowered her face to her hands. She'd run upstairs and waited until Rafi had left the entry area before she went down to the classroom. What the hell was wrong with her, flirting with Rafi?

The man was sex on two legs, and he was well aware of it. But that didn't stop her mouth from running away with itself. What would have happened if the reporter hadn't shown up and taken their picture?

She let out a groan. That was another thing. What would the rest of the royal family think, seeing her and Rafi's picture all over the gossip rags? Would her job be over before it started?

"Lady Bobbie," a male voice said.

Bobbie lowered her hands to see Hamaz standing in

the doorway with a plate in one hand and a glass of iced tea in the other. "Yes, Hamaz." She waved him into the room.

"Prince Rafi asked me to bring you a snack, and I thought you might like some iced tea to go with it." He walked in and set the items on the table.

"Thank you."

"Also, the first delivery has arrived. I will direct the delivery men to bring everything in here."

"That's fine, and Hamaz, you may call me Bobbie; there is no need for the lady."

Hamaz nodded, then left the room. Bobbie rose to her feet and pushed away her thoughts about Rafi and what had happened at the marketplace. She had a classroom to put together. Tonight would be soon enough to deal with her feelings about Rafi.

The next morning, Bobbie put her hands on her back, straightened, and let out a groan. Yesterday had been busy. The afternoon had been filled with the deliveries of the furniture and supplies. She'd spent time moving the tables where she wanted them. The delivery person told her the additional tables would arrive within a week.

Right now, that would work. She wanted to spend a few days just getting to know Zain before they started on a class routine. She'd spent the last two hours on the floor putting together several posters for the walls and now her back was protesting.

But she had three posters done. One for their morning routine, one for the afternoon routine, and a door covering. Bobbie bent down, lifted them off the floor, and laid them on one of the tables. She wrinkled her nose. She'd put them up this afternoon and then continue making more.

She glanced up as Hamaz arrived in the doorway. "What can I do for you, Hamaz?" Yesterday, he'd directed the deliveries and helped her move things where she wanted them.

"Another delivery has arrived."

"Oh, good, have them bring everything in." Yesterday had been the table, chairs, and some supplies. Today should be the rest of the supplies, the rug, and the beanbag chairs.

Within minutes men walked in carrying boxes, some big and some small. Bobbie directed them where to set them, but as they continued, she realized that not only was this the stuff she'd ordered in the marketplace, but her boxes from the United States had arrived as well.

By the time they were finished, about fifty boxes were stacked around the room. Bobbie rubbed her hands together. She had a lot of work in front of her, and she couldn't wait to get started. She opened the first box and started emptying the contents.

Rafi was so tired he couldn't see straight. Not only had he spent the rest of the previous day at the stables, but the previous night he'd gone out again. He'd been lucky to sneak back onto the palace grounds this morning with all the new security.

Khalid was training another batch of security personnel, and they'd been out early. Rafi apparently hadn't paid attention at the last meeting his brothers had had and almost got caught. Now, he'd spent most of the morning with the horses. All he wanted to do was shower and fall into bed but first he wanted ... no, needed to check in on one person.

He missed seeing Bobbie. He'd missed dinner last night because one of his mares had gone into early labor. Thank goodness everything was okay. Hamaz reported Bobbie was in her classroom unpacking boxes of supplies.

Turning down the hallway, he strode toward her classroom and through the door. "What the hell are you doing?" He didn't temper his voice. Bobbie was standing on a chair trying to put something on the wall.

At the sound of his yelled words, she pivoted and promptly lost her balance. Rafi ran across the room and steadied her before she fell.

"Rafi, you scared me." She glared down at him.

"Why are you standing on this chair?" His hands tightened around her hips as she turned and put the paper up on the wall.

"So I can get this poster up." She stretched her arms above her head and smoothed the top of the large paper in place. "You can let go now. I'm getting down."

"Turn around and put your hands on my shoulders." He didn't care his words were rough. He loosened his hold as she turned and put her hands where he wanted them. Then he lifted her off the chair, sliding her body down his as he set her on the floor.

He gazed down at her face as he held her close to him. Her hazel eyes held confusion and a hint of desire. Rafi fought against placing his lips against hers for several reasons. He was worried and angry at the same time.

"Why did you not ask Hamaz for help? You could have fallen off that chair and hurt yourself."

The desire was replaced with disbelief as she stiffened in his hold. "First off, I do this all the time, and second, I wouldn't have been in danger of falling except you scared me." She wiggled within his embrace.

"No more." His voice turned deeper. "Hamaz will help you or I will. No more climbing on chairs. It's too dangerous." What if someone else had scared her? Would they have been fast enough to catch her? If it had been Catherine, probably not. No, this was unacceptable. A shiver ran through his body as he gathered her even closer.

"Rafi," she wiggled. "You're crushing me. I need to breathe."

He relaxed his hold but still kept her in his arms. He was behaving irrationally but in his mind's eye all he could see was her tumbling off that chair. "I'm sorry, but I was worried."

"That's obvious, but there's no need to be." Her fingers ran over his cheek. "I decorate my classroom every year by myself. I'm always climbing on a chair or step stool."

Rafi frowned. "That is not acceptable. I will not have you injured." Images of what had happened when he was in college filled his mind. No, he wouldn't think about that. That was his past.

Her lips tilted up. "I've been doing this full time for five years now. Never once have I fallen while putting something up."

"It doesn't matter."

"Rafi." Her fingers smoothed over the lines on his forehead. "What can I do so you calm down?"

"Promise me you won't do it again."

She sighed, her warm breath caressing his skin. "I can't, because I know if one starts to fall or I need to put one up while teaching, I'll do it out of habit." He opened his mouth but she placed her fingers over his lips. "How about, I promise to do my best to get someone to help me?"

"If that is the best you can do," he said against her fingers.

"It is." He nodded, and she removed her fingers. "You smell of horses."

Rafi laughed. "I'm not surprised, I've been down with the horses. It is my job."

"I forgot." She leaned toward him. "I love the smell of horses."

"You do?" Rafi tilted his head, staring down at her.

"Yes, I grew up on a horse farm. I loved it."

The wistful tone in her voice intrigued Rafi. "What kind of horses?"

"Quarter horses. I used to help my dad." She let out a laugh. "If you could call it that. At seven, I was more interested in petting the horses than anything else."

"I bet you were." This was the first time she'd talked about her childhood. When he'd asked at dinner the other night she'd froze up. He chose his words carefully because he didn't want her to freeze up again. "Why don't I give you a tour tomorrow?"

"I'd like that, but I have a lot of work to do in here."

Rafi glanced around the room. There were boxes stacked up along one wall and empty broken-down ones on the floor. "How about a compromise?"

She tilted her head as she looked up at him. "What do you have in mind?"

"Tour in the morning and I'll help you here in the afternoon."

"I can't take you away from your work."

"But I'm taking you away from yours. This way we both get what we want."

"And what is it you want?"

"To be with you." The words slipped out without effort because they were true. He'd missed her, and he wanted to spend more time with her. Rafi wasn't sure how he was going to keep up with his nightly adventures, but he'd find a way. They were important. Important to the safety of his family and his people.

"Rafi." She said his name softly as her cheeks grew pink. "I don't know if that's a good idea."

"It is."

The clearing of a throat caused Rafi to turn his head to see his brother, Khalid, standing in the doorway. "Sorry to disturb you two."

"What is it?" Rafi could see the lines of strain on his brother's face.

"Malik would like to see you and Bobbie in his office."

"Me?" Bobbie squeaked out.

"Yes, Lady Bobbie, this concerns you too," Khalid said without giving anything away.

Rafi frowned at his brother, then turned back to Bobbie. "Might as well get this over with." Keeping an arm around Bobbie's waist, he guided her from the classroom to his brother's office.

She hesitated at the door, and Rafi squeezed her waist. "It will be fine," he whispered.

"What could the king want with me?" she whispered back.

Khalid opened the door for them, and Malik stood up behind his desk. "Thank you both for coming. Please sit."

Malik's face wasn't giving anything away. Khalid leaned against the wall as Rafi led Bobbie over to the chair and waited until she sat before he took a seat in the chair next to her.

Her hands fluttered into her lap, her fingers tangling together. Rafi's annoyance increased. "What's going on, Malik?"

"You would think after myself and Hassan, we would know how to deal with or at least avoid the press." He pushed a paper across the desk to Rafi.

Rafi picked it up and then he laughed. "I should have guessed," he said, staring at the picture of him and Bobbie at the café.

"What?" Bobbie looked over. "Oh, crap," she said, seeing the picture.

"It's very flattering," Rafi said. "We're staring at each other. We look quite in love."

"Nonsense." She looked at Malik. "I'm so very sorry. Should I pack?"

"What?" Malik said.

"No," Rafi said at the same time.

Her gaze bounced between the two of them and then Khalid chuckled. She glared at him. "This is nothing the family hasn't endured before," Khalid said.

"My brother is right," Malik said. "There is no reason for you to leave, but we're finding ourselves in a delicate position."

"I don't understand," Bobbie said.

Rafi could understand her confusion. She hadn't been around during Malik's and Catherine's courtship, let alone Hassan's and Sara's. "The paparazzi has a tendency to stalk the family when they get a whiff of one of us with a woman. They splash it over every newspaper they can and continue to stalk us."

"But we were just sitting there taking and having a snack." Bobbie's forehead wrinkled.

"The press will take it and twist it no matter what," Malik said. "We need to decide what the cover story will be."

"It's simple," Bobbie said. "I'm just here to teach Zain. That's what you tell them."

Rafi laughed. "Just like Catherine was here to paint the mural or Sara was here to support Catherine. Look at that picture, Bobbie. No one is going to believe you're here just to teach Zain."

"Damn it," she whispered.

"Rafi, what do you think?" Malik asked.

%   5   %

"Wait a second," Bobbie said. "I don't care what the press says. Zain is my priority, and I doubt Rafi and I will draw their attention."

"Want to bet?" Rafi whispered. "I'm crazy about you."

Heat filled her cheeks. "I've only been here a few days. No one is going to believe whatever story the press comes up with."

"You'd be surprised," Malik said rubbing his chin. He looked at his brother. "Khalid, what do you think?"

"The press is going to make up something no matter what, and Bobbie does have a point about only having been here a few days," Khalid said.

"I knew Catherine was for me after that first kiss, and I believe Hassan was the same way about Sara."

Bobbie shook her head. "This is insane." How could they think there was anything between her and Rafi? There wasn't. Yet.

"Sorry, Bobbie," Malik said. "No one expected the press to be in the marketplace on a Sunday."

Bobbie blinked. "It still doesn't matter. We're friends." At least right now. Yes, she was attracted to Rafi, but she was here to teach Zain, not become a royal plaything.

"You're scowling. Is being associated with me so abhorrent?" Rafi asked.

"No," she answered. It wasn't. "But I believe the people of Bashir are smart and will see through any story the press runs."

"Will they?" Rafi looked at his brothers. "Give us a minute."

The other men nodded and left the room. Rafi stood and pulled Bobbie with him. Her gaze met his, and she sucked in a breath at the desire burning in his dark eyes.

"I'm fine if you want the press to do their thing. But what if we release a story that says we're getting to know each other?" His voice was low and intoxicating. "This would give us the chance to be together without having to worry about who is seeing us. I want to explore this attraction to you." A grin teased his lips.

Bobbie wanted to give in to him, but fear held her back. She'd lost too many people she loved. Not that she loved Rafi that was crazy. They barely knew each other.

"What about you climbing the balcony and sneaking into the palace?"

The smile faded. "You cannot tell anyone about that."

"Why not? If we're going to do this, Rafi, I need to know the truth."

"There are factors at play I can't discuss at the moment." He cupped her cheeks with his palms. "But I promise you, what I'm doing is for the protection of my family and those in the palace."

She shook her head. "I'm just Zain's teacher." She pulled away from his hold. He didn't trust her and it hurt. But then, how much did she trust him? This was all too new.

Bobbie wasn't sure. She hardly knew him or anyone in the family. Heck, she hadn't even met Zain yet. She paced to the wall and back.

"Bobbie," Rafi started. "Are you willing to try?"

Her eyes widened. "This isn't fair, Rafi."

"No, the press intrusion isn't fair. Are you saying you're not attracted to me?"

"I am," she admitted. "I just ... " Her words trailed off as Rafi ran his fingers down her cheek, and she leaned into his touch. This was bad. Her reaction to him wasn't normal. "This is all happening so fast."

"We can go as slowly as you want, but the press is going to be there when we leave the palace grounds."

"And if we release a story that says we're seeing each

other?" Was she even thinking of doing this? She had to be out of her mind. She was nobody. She had no experience with royalty or being pursued by the press.

"The press will still be there, but not so hungry for a story. With that picture already circulating it's only going to cause more speculation."

Bobbie nodded. "If I agree to this, and I say if, it can't interfere with my work. Zain has to be my top priority."

"Not an issue. While you're with Zain, I'll be working with my horses."

Her stomach turned over. "Again, let me think for a bit. I'm going back to my classroom now." She walked over to the door and opened it.

Malik and Khalid stood there. "Gentlemen," she said and pushed past them. She needed to think. Bobbie turned down the hallway and realized she was lost again. Damn it, she needed to ask for a map.

Instead she found a door leading to the gardens. She pushed it open and walked out into the fresh air. She followed the winding path deeper into the garden. The scents of roses and jasmine filled the air.

What was she going to do? Flirting with Rafi was one thing, but exploring a relationship was another. She didn't have a good track record with men. Bobbie found herself by one of the big desert willow trees. She sat down beneath it out of the sun.

Mentally she began to do a list of pros and cons about this whole getting-to-know-you thing. The list was pretty even. It all came down to what she wanted. And that wasn't something she was sure of.

Bobbie leaned back against the tree trunk and looked up at the branches. Branches of life. The thought filtered through her head. Had she'd been living these last few years? Going through the motions, maybe.

That was one of the reasons she'd taken this job. To get her out of her rut and help her decide if she wanted to continue being a teacher. She loved helping kids, but a part of her wanted to put to use her vet tech license as well.

And then there was her love life. Laughter escaped. She didn't have one. She'd broken up with her last boyfriend more than a year ago because he'd found out she liked a little kink in the bedroom. The kink community in Seattle didn't fit her lifestyle, but she wanted to try it in her relationship.

Carl hadn't been very adventurous and when she'd mentioned him tying her wrists he freaked out. She hadn't expected that reaction. He called her a freak and ran out of her apartment.

He'd been another teacher at the school where she taught. After that, Carl wouldn't even talk to her when they passed each other at school, and later she'd heard the whispering about her. Apparently Carl couldn't keep his mouth shut, telling everyone she wanted to have forced sex, which wasn't even remotely true.

It had taken her a long time to come to terms with

wanting to be restrained during sex or even play. Carl's reaction had set her back. Bobbie was glad when the school year was over. She'd quietly quit and found another job with a private school, working with special-needs kids. She'd enjoyed that so much more. They were so eager to learn, and she was able to help them.

Like she wanted to help Zain. Catherine had explained about Zain's family, and while she and Malik wanted to adopt Zain, they couldn't, due to the rules of succession. For right now they were just taking care of Zain until something more permanent could be figured out.

Her mind circled back to Rafi and their present problem. She didn't want to cause any issues for the royal family, and even she had to admit that picture of her staring into Rafi's eyes could be mistaken for that of a woman in love.

She sighed. What would it hurt to explore this attraction with Rafi? It wasn't like she had anyone back home, and her life was pretty much an open book. And kink? Well, she'd been living without sex, let alone kink, for the last year. She could survive until she left Bashir.

Unless? Bobbie shook her head. What made her think Rafi might be into kink? Yeah, the man was dominant, protective, and forceful, but then all the men in this family seemed to be that way. With a grin on her lips, she pushed to her feet and made her way back to the palace.

Rafi paced around Bobbie's classroom. Where was she? She'd left Malik's office an hour ago, and he'd been unable to wait any longer for her answer. But when he entered her classroom she was nowhere to be found.

His first instinct was to raise the alarm, but he stopped himself. She could simply be in her room or out in the garden. Palace security had been tightened so there was no way she could leave the grounds without someone knowing and coming to tell him. He shook his head. Of course he could sneak out, but then he'd grown up here. He knew every nook and cranny. Would she agree to a relationship? This would be a way for him to spend time with Bobbie, and it would not be considered meat for the tabloid wolves.

Plus it would help keep his cover for those nights when he rode out into the desert to gather information. Others would assume he was in Bobbie's room and Bobbie herself?

A smile played around his lips. He was very interested in Bobbie. She intrigued him, but it was more than that. There was a natural attraction there. One he wanted to explore.

He stopped pacing when he came to the boxes. Well, since he was here, he could unpack these for her. Snagging the first box, he set it on the table and opened it. It was half-full of books.

Rafi pulled out the first one and turned it over. *Exploring the World of Kink*. The title leaped out at him. What the hell? He glanced in the box and realized these weren't schoolbooks but Bobbie's personal books.

So his Bobbie was interested in kink that was a plus. His fingers traced the title as his nerves danced with excitement.

"Rafi, what are you doing here?"

He dropped the book back into the box and turned to see Bobbie standing in the doorway. "Waiting for you."

"Oh." She stepped into the room. "I was out in the garden thinking." Her gaze went to the box. "That box should have been put in my bedroom." She stepped up next to him and pushed the lid closed. Her cheeks were flushed.

"Oh?" Did she realize he'd seen the first book?

"Those are my personal books." She pushed the box to the end of the table. "I'll have Hamaz carry it upstairs for me later."

"You have interesting reading choices," he said, keeping his tone neutral.

If anything her cheeks turned a deeper red. "You looked in the box?"

"I was planning on unpacking it for you so you wouldn't have to."

"Oh." She opened the box and peeked inside. Her eyes widened, and she slapped it closed. "I ... " Her hands fluttered against the cardboard.

"No need to be embarrassed." Rafi was more than intrigued, he wanted to find out just how far Bobbie was into kink.

"Ummm, maybe you should go."

"Maybe not." He trailed his fingers over her arm, watching as goosebumps spread over her flesh.

"Rafi." Her voice was breathless.

"I only saw the first book, but I wondered if there were others like that in the box." The flush on her cheeks now ran down her neck. "There's nothing to be embarrassed about."

"I ... ummm ... Oh, crap on a cracker."

Rafi laughed. "Crap on a cracker? Now, that's not an expression I've heard before."

"I use it when I don't want to swear. About the books."

"Yes." His thumb traced the pulse point in her wrist. "I'm very interested in that first book."

Bobbie swallowed. "You are?" Her eyes widened.

"Yep. Have you read it?" He kept rubbing her wrist, enjoying the feel of her skin beneath his thumb. Rafi watched her closely. Her breathing had increased, but she stayed relaxed in his hold.

She nodded and he smiled. "Good, then you're interested in kink," he said, whispering the last word.

"I ..." She nodded.

Rafi turned her into his embrace, enjoying the feeling of her in his arms. "I am too," he whispered.

Her mouth opened and then closed. He rested his

forehead against hers. "Just think of what we can explore together." He kept his tone soft and his hold gentle. He didn't want to frighten her.

"Rafi." Her breath brushed against his skin.

"I would love to explore with you, to find your likes and dislikes. To taste your lips once again." Bobbie trembled in his hold. "Does that frighten or excite you?" He didn't want her afraid.

"Excite." Her voice held honesty and eagerness.

"Good." He raised his head as he heard footsteps outside the classroom. "We'll talk more tonight about exploring together." He brushed a light kiss over her lips before releasing her and stepping back as Catherine walked into the room.

"Catherine." He glanced at Bobbie. "I'm going to go shower. See you ladies later." He turned and left the room.

Bobbie couldn't catch her breath. What had just happened? Desert storm Rafi. He battered down her defenses and was ready to raid the castle.

"Bobbie?" Catherine's voice penetrated the sensual spell Rafi had woven around her.

"Sorry, Catherine, what did you say?"

Catherine smiled. "I can see Rafi has been flirting again. He's such a scamp."

Bobbie laughed. "Scamp isn't quite the word I'd use."

"Yes, well, anyway. I thought if you could use some help, I'd help you unpack boxes."

"Oh, that's not necessary."

"Can I let you in on a secret?" Catherine's voice dropped.

"Of course."

"I'm hiding from the wedding planner."

Bobbie grinned. "That's right, your wedding is next month."

"Yes, and the planner is driving me nuts. I know this has to be a big state wedding and such, but I need a break."

"Then, by all means, you can hide in here." Bobbie moved the box on the table, made sure the flaps were sealed, and set it on the floor after. "But please sit. I can unpack the boxes myself."

"I want to help," Catherine said as Bobbie picked up a different box and set it on the table. She opened the lid and sighed in relief. School supplies.

"But ... " Bobbie wasn't sure it was proper for the future queen to open boxes and help her.

Catherine waved her hands in the air and reached into the open box. "I'll just sort all these out, and we can talk while we both unpack."

"Talk?" Bobbie's mouth grew dry.

"Yes. Tell me more about you and your life." Catherine began pulling out supplies.

Bobbie sighed and grabbed another box. "My life isn't very exciting."

"Tell me about Seattle, then. I was raised outside of London and moved to London when I was twenty. I bet Seattle is a lot like it."

"Seattle is wonderful," Bobbie said. "A large city with a very diverse population." Bobbie opened the box and began pulling out art supplies.

"Oh, my god, that's so funny," Catherine said two hours later.

"He really thought he could climb the space needle?" Sara asked.

Sara had joined them about thirty minutes after they'd started. Bobbie had been describing Seattle and life there. "Yep." She'd just finished telling them a story about a guy who decided to climb the space needle; he couldn't understand why they had arrested him. "It was funny, but not. Luckily no one got hurt."

"Can you imagine someone trying to climb the outside of Big Ben?" Sara said to Catherine.

"Yes, it's been tried."

The hours had flown by with Sara and Catherine to talk to. Bobbie found out how Catherine had come to Bashir to paint a mural for the children's ward at the hospital, only to fall in love with Malik.

Sara was a nurse who had taken some time off to help

Catherine with her wedding and then had fallen in love with Hassan.

Their relationships hadn't been easy. One of Malik's trusted advisors had tried to scare Catherine away, and Sara had been kidnapped by one of Kalif's men, but in the end all had worked out and they were very much in love.

Bobbie set another stack of books on the table. Among the three of them they'd unpacked most of the boxes. There was a set of boxes that needed to be taken to her room. "I think I'm going to need a bookcase or two and maybe a filing cabinet."

"No worries," Catherine said, "just order what you need. Oh, by the way, tomorrow they'll run an extension to the palace Wi-Fi in here so you won't have to worry about that."

"Oh, thank you. That's another thing, does Zain use any electronics right now?" She wasn't sure how much the boy had.

Catherine wrinkled her nose. "Not really. We have allowed him to use Malik's computer in his office, but we haven't gotten him anything."

"Would you mind if I ordered him a tablet? I will childproof it and give you and Malik the unlock codes."

"I don't see a problem with that," Catherine said.

"Are kids using tablets now in school?" Sara asked.

"In the States, yes. A lot of the schools prefer the kids to have them. It's easier for them to look things up, and at the last school I worked in, we had an electronic lending library for the kids. They used their tablets to read."

"I never thought about that," Catherine said.

"It's different. I still like books for the classroom, but it is much easier when you have copies electronically than worrying about the kids losing a paper book." Bobbie stacked the books. Tomorrow she'd start sorting them into a better system.

"Afternoon, ladies," Malik said from the doorway.

"Malik." Catherine jumped up and crossed the room. Malik pulled her into his arms and gave her a thorough kiss.

Bobbie looked over at Sara, who was smiling. "Don't mind them," she said.

Malik chuckled after he finished kissing Catherine. "I actually came to see Bobbie, but I see you're hiding out in here." He bopped his future wife on the nose with his finger.

"Just for a little while," she said.

"And I think it's time for Catherine and me to go see the wedding planner before she hunts us down." Sara crossed the room and linked her arm with Catherine's. "See you later, Bobbie." The two left.

"What can I do for you, Malik?" Bobbie brushed her hands down her jeans.

"I was wondering if you'd come to a decision?"

Bobbie almost asked what decision, then remembered their meeting from earlier today. "I'm still thinking. Can I give you an answer after dinner?"

Malik nodded, then glanced around the classroom. "This is starting to take shape. But ask for help if you need it."

"I will."

"Good."

After Malik left, Bobbie stood in the middle of the room hugging herself. She'd go shower and change for dinner. She still had that decision to make.

Bobbie sat down on the chair in Malik's office. She'd told him before dinner started she'd come to a decision, and he'd said they would discuss it after dinner. So now she, Malik, Khalid, and Rafi were all in the office.

"You said you'd come to a decision?" Malik asked after they were all settled.

"Yes." Bobbie swallowed. "I agree that we release to the press that Rafi and I are seeing each other." Her heart pounded at her words. There was no going back now.

"Thank you," Malik said.

Rafi took her hand in his. "I'll make things as easy as I can for you."

She nodded. "So what does this mean now?" She probably should have asked this question earlier, but once she'd made the decision, that was it. Bobbie was aware the decision would affect her life somewhat, but then again, she was only here for six months. At least according to her contract.

"It means a friendly appearance to show off the couple," Khalid said.

"Appearance?" Bobbie swallowed.

"Nothing major," Malik said. "Just a way for the people and the press to see you and Rafi together."

"Ten minutes tops," Khalid said.

"And being my date for Malik's and Catherine's wedding," Rafi added.

"Wedding?" Her gaze darted around the room. Oh, crap, she hadn't thought this through enough.

Malik nodded. "Right, if you two are seeing each other, of course you'll be his date."

"Please don't remind me of the wedding, it's a security nightmare," Khalid said.

"And you have it all under control," Malik countered.

Rafi squeezed her fingers, and she looked at him. "It will be okay," he whispered.

Bobbie nodded, but something told her that her life was going to take a turn she wasn't expecting.

"Well, now that we have that settled, I'm going to go spend some time with my soon-to-be wife." Malik stood.

Rafi helped her to her feet and guided her out of the room. He pulled her to a stop as the other two men strode down the hallway. "I'll be at your room in fifteen minutes."

"Why?"

"So we can discuss not only our relationship, but

kink." His voice was soft. Rafi brushed a kiss over her lips, then released her hand and strode away.

Bobbie's fingers touched her lips, and she sighed. Oh, why did he have to open that particular box? But even that thought didn't stop shivers of excitement from caressing her skin.

6

Bobbie paced around her room as she waited for Rafi. Was this something she wanted to do? Yes. Something about Rafi had called to her from the beginning. She wanted to explore what they could have together.

The whole thing with the press had thrown her for a loop, but after she thought about it, she came to the conclusion it was the best thing to do. Give the press their story, and then things would calm down. She didn't want the family to suffer just because she and Rafi had had their picture taken over coffee.

Hell, she needed to be honest with herself. She was more than attracted to Rafi. He revved her engines like a master mechanic.

A knock on her door caused her to jump. She walked

over and opened it a crack to see the man occupying her thoughts.

She pulled the door open, he stepped inside, and she closed the door. Before she could say a word, he pulled her into his arms, and his lips covered hers.

Her body melted against his. His lips pressed against hers, and his tongue darted out, tasting. She opened her mouth to him as one of his hands cradled her neck and his free arm encircled her waist.

Her tongue tangled with his. He tasted of mint and coffee, and she wanted more. Her arms entwined around his neck, her fingers sinking into his black hair.

It never crossed her mind to refuse his kiss. No, she'd been waiting for this ever since that first day on the balcony. His arm tightened around her, and her breasts pressed against his hard chest.

Her nipples tightened, and her nerves tingled with anticipation. He broke the kiss for a moment and she sucked in a breath, then his lips were back on hers. His mouth mastered hers and she let him.

This was what she needed, a man who would take charge. A man who could make her sensual side burn with pleasure and desire. Her thoughts almost had her pulling back. Where were these thoughts coming from?

"Rafi," she said his name softly, trying to catch her breath.

"So beautiful, so receptive, so sweet," he said, his lips trailing over her cheek to her ear.

His fingers on the back of her neck traced her skin lightly, sending shivers over her skin. Bobbie fought to get her breathing under control. This man could overwhelm her so easily.

"You said we would talk," she said.

"Talk, kiss, play." He nibbled at her skin.

Her breath caught in her throat. Oh, yes, she wanted to play. But they needed to talk first. She forced herself to release her hold on him. "Please," she said, pushing on his shoulders.

Rafi let out a breath, released her neck, loosened his hold on her waist, and took a step back. The moment he did she missed his heat. Then she bit her lip so as not to tell him to take her back into his arms.

"Let's go sit on the sofa," she said, fighting her own body. They did need to talk before they continued.

"Very well."

Bobbie led the way and Rafi followed, sitting next to her.

"Am I overwhelming you?" He pushed a piece of her hair away from her face.

"A bit." Just as she got her breathing under control, he touched her and it went crazy once again. "It's been a while since I've been in a relationship."

"For me as well."

She laughed. "Why don't I believe that?"

Rafi frowned. "It is true. I haven't dated a woman in over a year."

"Why? Are women here blind?" Bobbie couldn't believe Rafi hadn't dated in a year. He was handsome and sexy.

"No. It is not easy when you're a member of the royal family," he said, sitting back with a sigh.

"I'm sorry," she whispered. "I never thought of that." She'd forgotten he was royal. "We've never really discussed your family."

"True." He glanced over at her. "I'm the second son, but now that Malik has become king and is about to marry Catherine, I don't have to worry about the throne."

"Why not?" She was curious.

"Because once they start having children, their children will be in line for the crown."

"And you're okay with that?"

"Oh, yeah." Rafi gave her one of his sexy grins. "I never really wanted to be king. I like my horses."

"But you want kids someday?" Her stomach clenched.

"Yes, but I don't see that happening for a while."

Bobbie closed her eyes and then opened them. Time to change the subject to something else. "Tell me about working with the horses. How did you get into that?"

"I used to sneak out to the stables when I was supposed to be learning. Our stable manager took pity on me and began teaching me. Horses were easier to deal with than protocols and all the stuffiness that came with being royal."

Bobbie tilted her head. If there was one thing this

family wasn't, it was stuffy. They were the most down-to-earth people she'd ever met. "I wouldn't consider any of you stuffy."

"Mainly because of our mother." Rafi's features softened. "Mom and Dad are at the summer palace right now in the west. But when you meet my mom, you'll understand."

Bobbie nodded. "So Malik is the oldest, you're second, then Hassan, and Khalid is the baby?"

"Yep, although don't let Khalid hear you say he's the baby, especially since he's in charge of security."

"You all have different responsibilities."

"Yes, but Malik has always been groomed to be king. I had some training, but not as much, and Hassan and Khalid were allowed to have minimal."

"Tell me more."

"I'd rather talk about more intimate things." His finger traced over her cheek. "Tell me more about you. When was your last relationship?"

"Over a year ago."

"So long. I suspect it's not because you weren't interested."

"Yes and no." She almost captured his fingers against her cheek to keep his touch against her skin, but she held herself back. Why was she so needy all of a sudden? This wasn't like her. "I had offers, but I wasn't really interested."

He nodded. "And kink?"

Her stomach turned over. How did she explain it? "I'll try to explain. I discovered the kink community when I was nineteen. You see, the day I turned eighteen my mother threw me out."

"What?" Rafi almost yelled. "Your mother abandoned you?"

"Not by her standards." Bobbie surged to her feet. She rarely talked about her past, but if she and Rafi were going to have a relationship he had to know some of her history. "My mother decided at eighteen I was an adult and I could take care of myself. When I was nineteen I was going to school for my teaching certificate and working a part-time job." She'd kept her voice calm and her tone neutral. Inside her stomach churned. She focused instead on the job she'd held during that time. The job at a local pizza place had been a lifeline and was fun with flexible hours.

"Go on." He watched as she paced.

"Well, there was a group that came in every month to use the banquet area. I got to know some of the people. It turned out it was a local kink group that held a lunch there every month."

"A good group of people?"

"Yes." Her lips turned up. "They were fun, always friendly and tipped well." She stopped pacing and sat back down. "Master Dan, the overall dominant, and I began talking one night. He explained to me who they were and what they were about. I was curious and began asking him questions."

"And did he answer all your questions?"

"Yes. Master Dan was great. He introduced me to other people, and if I was working whenever they came in, they requested I be their waitress." Master Dan had found a way to help her without taking her independence away; she appreciated that.

"Were you and Master Dan lovers or just play partners?"

Bobbie's eyes widened. "Neither." Then she let out a laugh. "Master Dan was in his fifties. He took me under his wing and helped me understand."

Rafi frowned as if trying to figure out what she was saying.

"Master Dan was a teacher at heart. He saw my curiosity and taught me the rights and wrongs in the kink community. He taught me how to recognize a predator versus a Dom looking for a sub."

"Now I understand. A mentor."

"In a way, yes. He would stay with me when I went to the club, and he let everyone know I was under his protection."

"A very good Dom," Rafi whispered. "How often did you play?"

"I've only played a few times." She tangled her fingers together. "I'm not comfortable playing in public."

"Some aren't and there's nothing wrong with that. I prefer to keep it private as well."

"Have you been to a club?"

"Once in London; it was all right, but like you, I wasn't comfortable with what I was seeing in public." He rubbed her arm. "Tell me what you like?"

Bobbie blew out a breath. "I like being restrained. I've played with toys and have enjoyed a spanking or two." Would he think she was too odd? She didn't think so. He didn't react to the book in a negative fashion, more like he was intrigued.

"Have you tried bondage?" His fingers skimmed over her cheek before he cupped her chin and turned her face to his. His dark eyes were alight with desire.

"Not really. Usually someone just holding my hands or gripping the back of my neck." She swallowed. Her blood heated at the thought of being tied up and at his mercy.

"Something we can explore together," he said, his warm breath brushing over her face. "Safewords?"

She shook her head. "I've never had a reason to use them." Her play had been restricted to those she trusted even if it didn't always turn out so well.

"You should always have safewords, no matter what. Give me two words that you would never call out during a sexual encounter."

Bobbie wrinkled her nose as she thought. "Bronco and harness." Those were the first two words that came to mind.

Rafi laughed. "Interesting words, but they will work. Bronco if you want me to stop, harness to slow down."

She nodded. "Why do we need safewords?" She vaguely remembered Master Dan saying something about them, but since she didn't like to play in public she didn't pay a lot of attention.

"Because if I do something that scares you I need to know." He moved closer to her. "Do you not know about safewords?"

"I've heard about them but I never really paid attention."

"Well, now you will." He stared at her. "As your dominant it is my responsibility to make sure you are safe even when we are playing."

"What makes you think I'm submissive?" She wanted to know how he thought. It didn't matter that her insides melted at his commanding tone.

His fingers tangled in her hair, pulling her head back with a firm tug. Her breath became rapid, and if she hadn't been seated, her knees would have given out.

"You like that?" His dark eyes sparkled as he shifted on the sofa.

"Yes," she whispered. She didn't understand what was happening to her. She didn't like it when other men had grabbed her hair. But there was something different with Rafi. He wasn't harsh. While his fingers were tangled in her hair, and she could feel the firmness of his grip, it wasn't punishing. And if she said the word, he'd let her go.

How did she know that? Because on a certain level she trusted him. He'd been open and honest with her so far. Well, all except about his climbing the balcony and what he'd been doing.

She'd give him a little slack on that. He was adamant he was protecting his family and people.

"Your reaction is so amazing. Your breathing has sped up and your skin is flushing, all from my hand in your hair," he said. "So sweet, so beautiful, so submissive." He brushed his lips across hers. "I can't wait to play with you."

"We're not going to play tonight?"

Rafi shook his head. "No. Tomorrow will be a busy day with the public outing and probably answering questions from the press. You need to be rested."

The desire Bobbie had been feeling fled with the thoughts of facing the press. "Was this really the only way out?"

"Are you having doubts?"

"A few. I'm not very comfortable in front of the press."

"I'll be right there with you, and you don't have to say anything. I can do all the talking."

"You'd do that for me?" A sense of safety filled her.

"Of course. You are being dragged into something not of your making. I will do everything in my power to take care of you."

The words, take care of you, set her nerves on edge but she reined in her annoyance. Rafi wasn't trying to take away her independence. A knock on her door caused her to jump. "Who could that be?"

Rafi removed his hold, stood, and crossed the room. He opened the door. "Oh, hello, Sara," he said.

"Rafi," Sara's soft voice carried across the room. Bobbie stood. Rafi held the door open, and Sara entered, carrying a white bag over her arm. She smiled at Bobbie. "Hi, Bobbie, I promise it won't take long. Malik asked if I'd come and help you."

"I think that is my signal to leave." Rafi strode back over to Bobbie. "Until tomorrow." He grasped the back of her neck, and his lips covered hers.

Without thought, Bobbie entwined her arms around his neck as her lips parted and their tongues tasted each other. Her blood sang even as he broke the kiss. "Sleep well, sweetheart," Rafi said, and then he swept out of the room.

"I always knew Rafi was hot, but damn, that kiss just about caught the room on fire," Sara said.

Bobbie stared at Sara for a moment, then burst out laughing. "Why did Malik send you?" she asked.

"Because Catherine still isn't comfortable with the press, and I know how to handle them. Plus I thought it would be nice for me to take you under my wing as Catherine did for me." Sara laid the white bag over the back of the sofa. "I promise it won't take long. Just some tips, and of course, your outfit for tomorrow." Sara patted the bag.

"Outfit?" Bobbie swallowed. She was more a jeans or long skirt type of person.

"Yes, don't worry. It's very modest and perfect for you." Sara grinned. "Now let's discuss what is going to happen."

Rafi paced around the anteroom outside the press room. The announcement had gone out in the morning papers, and the craziness had begun. He'd escaped to the stables early this morning, leaving Malik and Khalid to deal with the crap. Now, he was dressed in his royal robe, waiting for Bobbie.

"You're nervous," Khalid said.

"A bit." It was rare for him to be this unsettled.

"Bobbie is an intelligent, thoughtful woman. She suits you."

"Yes, but this isn't the way I wanted to court her."

"So you are interested."

Rafi's hackles went up. "Yes. What made you think I'm not?"

"Nothing." Khalid shook his head. "It just surprises me how women coming to do a job or visit are suddenly part of our family."

Rafi grinned. "It is a different way to find wives. First Catherine and the mural, then Sara visiting Catherine and now Bobbie."

"And you know the press is going to make the connection."

Rafi hadn't thought of that. He would need to be prepared for those types of questions. "Probably, but the cover story of us seeing each other should be enough."

Khalid shook his head. "The press will eat up the 'love at first sight' type of relationship."

"Let's hope so." Rafi stopped talking as Khalid's eyes widened. Rafi turned and his mouth went dry.

Bobbie stood there in an intricately designed caftan trimmed with the royal colors, her dark hair piled high on her head and also decorated with ribbons in the royal colors. Her hazel eyes sparkled with nervousness.

"Bobbie," Rafi said her name on a sigh. "You are so very beautiful." He crossed to her and took her hands in his. They were ice cold. He frowned.

"Thank you." Her voice trembled.

"It will be okay." Rafi drew her closer to him. "I will take care of you. You have nothing to be worried about."

She nodded but he could still see the apprehension in her eyes. He wanted to kiss her to wipe all those fears away, but this wasn't the place or time.

"If you're ready," Khalid said.

Rafi brushed a kiss over her cheek, then turned, keeping one hand in his. "We're ready."

Khalid nodded and then opened the door to the press room. Rafi guided Bobbie through the door. She stiffened at the room full of press, but he kept her moving until they stood before the podium.

"Thank you all for coming today." His voice was clear and strong. "As you are aware," he paused to gaze down at Bobbie before continuing, "pictures of Bobbie and I were taken outside the café in Bashir City, and before you go crazy, yes, we are seeing each other."

To Bobbie's credit, she didn't flinch as the flashes from the camera began going off and the room filled with voices.

"Why the quick announcement?" yelled a male reporter.

"Haven't you ever heard about love at first sight?" Rafi quipped. He squeezed Bobbie's hand.

"But Miss Anderson has only been in Bashir, what, four days?" another reporter said.

Bobbie stiffened beside him. "True. But again, I knew from the moment I saw her I wanted to pursue a relationship with her."

The volume in the room went up. "Really, Prince Rafi?" a female reporter said. "You're known for being a big flirt."

Bobbie glanced up at him, and he captured her gaze with his. "My past is my past; this is the woman I want in my life," he said. "Forever," he whispered to her. In his heart this was the right thing. She called to him on a level he'd never felt before. It might be considered love, but for the moment he wasn't going to give it a name. All he knew was he wanted her with him, by his side, in his life and his bed.

She lifted her hand and cupped his cheek. Without conscious thought, he cupped her chin, lowered his head, and brushed a kiss over her lips. He barely heard the camera clicks, but the flashes caused him to close his eyes for a minute.

When he broke the kiss, Bobbie sighed. He fought against sweeping her into his arms and carrying her to his room where they could be alone.

"Prince Rafi, how did you two meet?"

A shudder went through her body, and Rafi tucked her close to his side before turning back to face the reporters. "Bobbie is here to be Zain's teacher."

"Does that mean King Malik and Crown Princess Catherine are going to adopt Zain?"

"How does that affect the succession?"

"How soon can we expect your wedding?"

The questions were shouted, and with each one, Bobbie pressed closer to his side. Khalid stepped forward.

"As for the adoption of Zain, right now the king and crown princess are discussing things with the advisors and tribal leaders. Zain is currently under their care and will stay that way until a decision is made. As for Rafi and Bobbie's wedding," Khalid glanced at them, "don't you have enough to do with the king's wedding upcoming?"

Murmurs filled the room. "Thank you, brother," Rafi said.

"I suggest we conclude this now."

Rafi nodded. "Now, if you'll all excuse us, there is nothing more to say." Rafi guided Bobbie out of the room even as reporters shouted and flashes went off. The second they were clear of the room, Bobbie sagged against him.

"Is it always like that?" she asked.

"Yes," Catherine said, walking up to the pair. "Bobbie, are you okay?"

Rafi looked down at Bobbie's pale face. Maybe this hadn't been his best idea.

"I'll be fine," she said, giving Catherine a little smile, then she glanced up. "Sara, thank you for helping me last night and this morning. I really didn't expect the reporters to be so curious."

Sara gave a laugh. "You'll get used to it."

"They're vultures," Catherine muttered.

Khalid laughed. "They can be, but for now they'll have to be satisfied with this tidbit. If you'll all excuse me, I have to go meet with my security teams. Keeping everyone safe is a challenge." Khalid turned and walked away.

"Is your safety an issue?" Bobbie asked, her eyes filled with concern.

"Not usually," Rafi answered.

"We've just had some issues of late," Sara said, her hands waving in the air. "But Khalid is good at what he does, and he's hired lots of security to make sure everyone is safe. That includes you now."

"Yes, it does. I'm having Hamaz assigned to you," Rafi said.

"I don't need a bodyguard," Bobbie said, raising her chin.

"And I think that's our clue to leave," Catherine said, linking her arm with Sara's, and they walked away.

"I need to make sure you are safe."

"Are you saying I'm not safe in the palace?"

"You are."

"Then I don't see the issue."

Rafi let out a sigh. He remembered thinking how funny it was when Catherine and Sara argued with his brothers about their security. Now he wasn't finding it so funny. "Can we compromise?"

"How?"

"If you leave the palace, you take Hamaz with you. He will always be available for you."

Bobbie tilted her head and then nodded. "I can live with that."

"Thank you." He brushed a kiss over her cheek. "Why don't we go get changed, and I'll take you down to the stables?"

"Now?"

"Yes, I promised you a tour. After we're done we can have lunch, then I'll help you with your classroom."

Her eyes brightened. "It will only take me a few minutes to change." Excitement filled her voice, and Rafi found his lips turning up. It took so little to make her happy.

"Then let's go."

$$\sim$$

Bobbie hung the beautiful robe in her closet and let out a sigh. She normally wasn't a timid person, but those reporters had scared the crap out of her. While Sara had warned her about them, having to face them in reality had been so much different.

But still she'd survived. She pulled on a pair of jeans and then a light blouse before rummaging through her closet for a pair of boots. She'd packed a pair hoping she could get some riding in while she was here.

She missed being on a horse. She rode when she could in Seattle, but it wasn't as often as she'd like. Her heart squeezed. She missed her father and their horse ranch. She pushed away her sad thoughts and locked them back up. She didn't have time to dwell on the past, only to deal with the here-and-now and maybe the future.

Bobbie tugged on her boots as a knock sounded on her door. Crossing the room, she opened the door and her mouth went dry.

Rafi stood there in black riding pants, black boots, and a white shirt, all molded to his perfect body. Damn, this man was sexy.

"Ready?" he asked as his gaze scanned her. "Oh,

good, you have boots. I was going to try to find you a pair if you didn't."

"I do." She stepped out of her room and shut the door behind her. That was when she noticed Hamaz standing off to the side. "Hello, Hamaz."

"Lady Bobbie." Hamaz inclined his head.

"I thought you said I would only need Hamaz if I left the palace alone."

"Yes, but he's coming with us today so you get used to having him around." Rafi cupped her elbow.

It was something Bobbie noticed, that he was constantly touching her, guiding her. It was a bit disconcerting until she came to the conclusion it was a part of who he was. She'd noticed it with his brothers as well with Catherine and Sara. They were always making sure they were safe.

"So, how many horses do you have?" she asked as they walked to the stables.

"Six stallions right now, four mares, and one new foal," Rafi said.

"All Arabians?"

"Yes. They are the best horses."

They stepped inside the long stable. There had to be at least twenty stalls. "Impressive," she said.

Rafi clicked his tongue and horses' heads came out of the stall doors. Bobbie clasped her hands. "They're so beautiful."

"They are." He led her over to one of the horses.

"This is Shadow. He's my personal horse." Rafi reached out and ran his hand over the horse's nose.

"Hey, Shadow." Bobbie held her hand out, letting the horse sniff it, before she stroked her hand down his withers. "His coat is so soft." She continued stroking him.

"I keep him brushed along with the other horses."

Shadow blew out air from his nose, and Bobbie laughed as he pushed against her hand.

"He likes you," Rafi said.

"Are the other horses here for the family to ride?"

"No. These are my breeding horses. The rest of the family horses are in the other stable."

"You have two stables?" Heck, when her father had had his place, he'd only had one stable, smaller than this. Most of the horses were left to roam the fields. "Do they not run the grounds?"

"They do." He guided her away from Shadow. "They're let out every day, but most come back for lunch, then go and run again."

"Interesting. How often do you breed the mares? Do you sell the offspring?"

"You're full of questions." He took her hand in his and turned her to face him. "I'll explain our operation."

Rafi couldn't remember when he'd spent a more fun day. After taking Bobbie to the stables and explaining his operation, they'd had lunch and he'd gone back with her to her classroom. He hung up the posters she'd made and helped her make more.

While he and his brothers had had private tutors when they were children, none of them were like Bobbie, and he didn't remember the classroom being decorated. After the posters were hung, he separated markers, crayons, colored pencils, and other crafty things into different colored mini-baskets, while she set up books, writing paper, craft paper, and heavy drawing paper in their respective places. As they worked, Rafi learned a bit more about Bobbie. She still didn't talk much about her childhood, but she told him about college.

He told her about going to college, getting his degree in equine science. How he loved being around the horses. How when he'd first started, the old stable master would take him to task for the littlest mistake, but as soon as Rafi showed he wasn't afraid of hard work, he started teaching Rafi more and more.

"Shortly after I graduated college, old Tazman had a heart attack. He realized he couldn't go on and passed everything on to me," he finished his story.

"You really enjoy working with the horses," she said, straightening the last stack of books.

"Yes, when I was a child they were my escape from everything."

Bobbie's hazel eyes clouded with confusion. "Were you unhappy as a child?"

"Not unhappy, so to speak. As the second child, I still had to take some of the protocol classes Malik did. I hated them. I wanted to be out in the desert riding my horse."

"And he did it as often as he could," a male voice said from the doorway.

"Father." Rafi rushed to the doorway and hugged the man. "We weren't expecting you and Mom back for another week."

"Yes, well, we saw your press conference and had to come home to see what was going on." He peered around his son's shoulder.

"Bobbie." Rafi turned and held out his hand, grateful when Bobbie crossed the room and put her hand in his. "This is my father, Jamal. Dad, Bobbie."

"Sir." Bobbie gave a slight curtsey.

"No formalities." Jamal waved his hand. "It's nice to meet you, Bobbie. May I call you that?"

"Yes, please. I'm happy to meet Rafi's father."

"Where is Mother?" Rafi asked, looking into the hallway.

"She's grilling Malik."

"Oh, no," Bobbie whispered. "Is this relationship causing a problem?"

"I'm more interested in how this relationship got started and why it was announced?" His father's tone was sharp, and his gaze swung to Rafi.

"I can explain," Rafi started.

"Well, you'd better, because your brother isn't making

much sense," an older female voice said. "Oh, now, this is a classroom."

Rafi shook his head. "Bobbie, this is my mother, if you haven't already figured it out."

"Hello, dear." His mother took Bobbie's hand in hers as she looked Bobbie over. "Hmmm, you'll do."

Bobbie looked at Rafi and he shrugged his shoulders.

"I'm sorry you cut your vacation short, ma'am," Bobbie said. "I hope you aren't too upset over this turn of events."

"Nonsense. I was more concerned about what my second son had done to warrant an announcement." She glared at Rafi.

"He didn't do anything," Bobbie said quickly. "It wasn't his fault. We were just sitting at the café when the press took our picture."

"Bobbie," Rafi started.

"No, I won't allow anyone to blame you for something you couldn't control."

"Oh, yes, she'll fit in quite nicely," Rafi's mother said.

"What?" Bobbie shook her head.

"I'll explain later." Rafi raised her hand to his mouth and kissed the back of it. "As Bobbie said, we were at the café in the marketplace when a reporter took our picture. It ended up being in the paper."

"And you thought announcing you're in a relationship was the answer?" His mother put her hands on her hips, glaring at her son.

"Yes." He wasn't going to apologize for doing what he'd done. "It will protect Bobbie but also give us a chance to get to know each other better without interference."

"We raised our sons right," his mother said, looking at his father. "I expect to see both of you at dinner. We have a lot to discuss." With that, his parents walked away.

Bobbie looked up at him. "What was that about?"

"That was a sandstorm called my mother." He brushed his fingers over her cheek. "We better go get ready for dinner."

"Do I need to wear something special?" she asked as he led her away from her classroom and toward their rooms.

"Just be you." And he had no doubt she'd already won his parents over by her defense of him.

❧ 7 ☙

Bobbie laughed as Anna told a story about Rafi and Hassan going out into the desert to live like their ancestors had. "Oh, you must have been so worried."

"Yes, and no." She waved her hands at her two sons. "Their bodyguards were with them, and we knew they would come home when they got hungry enough."

"That's for sure," Hassan said with a smile. "It's a good thing I already told Sara this story, or she'd go running for the hills."

"Never," Sara said, patting his hand.

Bobbie noticed the way the couple looked at each other, and she fought back a sigh. That was the kind of love she wanted, but deep inside she was aware it could never happen. She was broken inside.

Her stomach turned over, and she forced her thoughts

back into their box where they belonged. She wanted to enjoy dinner and being with Rafi.

"It was more difficult to catch food than we thought it would be," Rafi said with a grin.

"More like impossible," Hassan muttered, and everyone laughed.

"Any mishaps when you were a child, Bobbie?" Anna asked.

Bobbie thought for a moment. "There was this one time, I was eight and I decided to bake a cake for my dad for his birthday." A grin teased her lips as she remembered.

"Did you know how to cook?" Catherine asked.

"Nope, but that wasn't going to stop me." Laughter came easier now. "When my mom came into the kitchen she lost it. I was covered head to toe with flour, and there were ingredients everywhere. I just smiled and told her the cake was in the oven."

"What did she do?" Sara asked.

"She marched me upstairs and into a bath and told me to clean up, and that she'd watch my cake. I didn't find out until I was older my cake was inedible, but my mom whipped up another one quickly and passed it off as mine."

"That was sweet of her," Anna said.

"Yes, it was." Her mother had been so different when she was little and her father was alive. After her father had died, Bobbie realized her mother couldn't function well without him. She'd only gone through the motions until Bobbie was eighteen. A touch of sadness filled her. If her father hadn't been a risk-taker, her life might have been much different.

Rafi's warm touch against the skin of her hand where it rested on the table brought her back to the present. "Are you okay?" he asked softly. She nodded.

"Are your parents still living?" Anna asked.

"My father died when I was sixteen." She took a deep breath at the familiar pain. "My mother, I honestly don't know. I haven't seen her since I was eighteen."

Anna's eyes widened, and Jamal shook his head. Shame filled Bobbie. She started to push back her chair to excuse herself when Rafi placed his arm behind her, trapping her at the table.

"You have nothing to be ashamed of," Rafi said quietly. "What Bobbie didn't say is her mother kicked her out when she was eighteen." He squeezed her shoulder in support.

"How did you know?" She gazed into his dark eyes, which were filled with compassion and understanding.

"Because I'm getting to know you." He leaned over and brushed a kiss over her nose.

"Well, let's talk about something else," Anna said. "Catherine, how is the wedding coming? Only three weeks until the big day."

Bobbie was glad to have the attention off of her. She let the conversation of the wedding flow over her as her nerves settled and she finished eating. Maybe one day her parents' abandonment wouldn't hurt so much.

Rafi turned Shadow to the northeast with the moon as his light. He'd wanted to spend the night with Bobbie, but he needed to check out the latest Intel about Kalif's men being in one of the northeast villages close to Bashir City.

He was well aware his brothers wouldn't approve of his late-night wanderings, but Rafi wanted to do something to help capture Kalif and rid their country of the opium problem.

A mile from the village, he dismounted and left Shadow to rest and graze at one of the lush outcroppings. He continued on foot to the village. Rafi kept to the shadows. Even though he was dressed in black, he didn't want to alert anyone to his presence.

It was late and the town was quiet, but there was one building that was lit up. Rafi crept closer. He carefully looked inside one of the windows. Six men sat around smoking opium. Squatting, he listened to what was being said.

Rafi yawned as he brushed Shadow. "Rest well, my friend." Rafi patted the horse before closing the stall door behind him and making his way to the palace. He'd write up his findings and make sure they made their way to Khalid, anonymously, of course.

If his family ever found out what he was doing they would be furious, especially Khalid, who took the family security seriously. Rafi understood, but he needed to do something to help, and he was good at sneaking around. Too many dismissed him as the fun prince, the unserious one.

He'd cultivated that impression over the years. It allowed him a certain freedom but also allowed him to hear things others didn't want the royal family to know about. He made his way into the palace, nodding at the guards, who were used to him being in the stables at all times of the night, and climbed the stairs to his room.

As he neared his room he noticed a light on in Bobbie's room. Why wasn't she asleep? Opening his bedroom door, he went inside and put away his black robe and headdress, then he went to her door and knocked softly.

After a moment, he heard movement from the room. "Who is it?" she asked, her voice quiet.

"Rafi."

The door opened and he slipped inside. "Why aren't you asleep?" he asked.

"I could ask you the same thing." She shut the door and stared at him.

Rafi didn't have an answer for her. He couldn't tell her

what he really had been doing. And since she had been at the stables today, he didn't think she'd buy that he was checking on his horses. "I couldn't sleep, so I took a walk in the garden."

"I couldn't sleep either." She gestured to the sofa.

Rafi wasn't convinced about her not sleeping. Something was off. "Bobbie," he started, but she put her fingers to his lips.

"I'm having a bad night, Rafi. I have no right to ask, but would you hold me?"

Her soft plea tugged at his heart. "You have every right to ask." He pulled her into his arms and kept her in his lap as he sat on the sofa. "What is wrong?"

"Memories," she whispered, laying her head on his shoulder.

Rafi understood. There were nights when memories of the explosion a month ago still woke him from his dreams, and then there were all the mishaps with Catherine. And Sara's almost kidnapping. While none of them had happened to him personally, it affected his family, his brothers.

"Did my family press too much tonight?" He stroked her raven hair.

"No, they wanted to know, and it was okay. It's ..." She tilted her head back so she could look at him. "It hurts. I miss my dad so much."

The tears filling her eyes punched him low in the stomach. "Sweetheart." He tightened his hold around her.

"I know it's been more than ten years, but I still don't understand it."

Rafi was about to ask how her father had died but then decided not to. He'd just let her talk or cry, and he'd hold her for as long as she'd like.

Bobbie didn't want to wake up. She snuggled into the warmth surrounding her. It had been too long since she'd felt this safe, this cared for. The memories of the previous night flooded her brain, and she forced her eyes to open.

She was cradled against Rafi's chest, and he was still sound asleep. This gave her a chance to study him, to see if she could figure this complicated man out. Because he was complicated, even if others didn't think so.

Maybe tonight they would be able to play together. She was excited to see how well she and Rafi fit together. Bobbie let out a sigh. While she wanted to play with Rafi, she knew a relationship with him couldn't go anywhere. She was broken inside and nothing could fix her.

"That was a big sigh. Are you okay?" Rafi asked.

Bobbie tilted her head up and gazed into his dark eyes. "I'm fine. I'm just hoping we have some time tonight, alone."

He grinned. "I'll have to see what I can do. In the meantime ... " He lowered his head and his lips captured hers.

She allowed herself to sink into the kiss, to enjoy the feel of his lips against hers. All too soon he was lifting his head.

"Someone is knocking at your door."

Her eyes widened. "I don't know who it can be. It's Saturday." Bobbie worked her way out of Rafi's hold and grabbed her robe from the chair. "I'll be right back."

"Wait." Rafi climbed off the mattress and pulled on his pants. "I'm going with you."

Bobbie's hands fluttered in the air. "But … " She didn't know what she was going to say.

"No one will think anything about my spending the night in your room." Rafi grasped her elbow and gently led her from the bedroom. When they were close to the door Rafi released her and reached for the knob.

Her stomach churned as he opened the door. "Oh, hi, Rafi," Catherine's bubbling voice floated into the room. "Is Bobbie awake?"

Rafi opened the door all the way and gestured for Catherine to enter. "Good morning, Catherine, what's up?" Bobbie said.

"Sorry to bother you. I know it's Saturday, but for once I have the morning free, and I thought maybe you might like to spend some time with Zain."

"I'd love to. Can you give me like, thirty minutes to get ready?"

"No worries." Catherine waved her hand. "Take your time. We're just now going down to breakfast, so join us when you can." Catherine looked at Rafi. "And you too, you're spending way too much time at the stables again." With that Catherine turned and walked out of the room.

Rafi closed the door and shook his head.

"What did she mean, spending too much time at the stables?" Bobbie asked.

"My family always seems to think I spend too much time with my horses, but now I have a reason not to." He stepped up to her and cupped her face. "I guess we both better get ready and go down to breakfast or Catherine will hunt us down."

Bobbie's skin heated at his touch. "I guess so." While she'd rather spend more time with Rafi, she did have a job to do.

"Tonight. I promise." He brushed a soft kiss against her lips before he turned and left the room.

Bobbie sighed and then made her way to the bathroom. Tonight, she promised herself. Tonight she would be able to play with Rafi.

Rafi walked into the breakfast room. Catherine, Malik, and Zain were the only ones at the table. He poured himself a cup of coffee, then picked up a plate and filled it with food before sitting down at the table.

"I thought Bobbie would be here by now," he said.

"I'm sure she'll be here any second," Catherine said with a twinkle in her eye.

"Good morning, everyone," Bobbie's cheerful voice filled the room as she walked in. Rafi and Malik automatically stood, and she waved her hands at them. "Please sit back down."

Malik resumed his seat but Rafi crossed over to her. "Good morning again, sweetheart." He brushed a kiss over her cheek. "Let me get your coffee. You get your food."

Bobbie's hazel gaze met his. There was confusion in her eyes, but he just winked at her and got her a cup of coffee, adding cream and sugar before carrying it to the table. He waited until she sat down with her food before he resumed his own seat.

"I don't think I've been introduced to this handsome young man," Bobbie said.

"Bobbie, this is Zain. Zain, this is Lady Bobbie; she is going to be your teacher," Malik said in a soft tone.

"Hello, Zain. I am so happy to meet you." Bobbie held out her hand.

Zain looked at Catherine and then Malik before he took Bobbie's hand and gave it a little shake.

Bobbie noticed Catherine blinking back tears. She wasn't surprised that Zain didn't say anything to her. She'd been informed of his quietness. She sat back in her chair and began eating, letting the conversation flow over her.

All the while, she watched Zain. The little boy was

aware of everything going on around him. His gaze would go to whomever was speaking even as he ate his breakfast. While he might have issues with talking, Bobbie had a suspicion he was highly intelligent. She would have to test that out.

"Well, now that we're done with breakfast," Catherine said, "why don't we go see Bobbie's classroom?"

Zain's brown eyes grew wide, but he nodded. Everyone stood, but Bobbie waited until Zain was close to her. She knelt down so she could see into the little boy's eyes and said, "I'm very happy to be here and teaching you, Zain. I think you'll like your classroom, and I'm more than happy to show it to you." Bobbie held her hand out to the little boy.

The room went silent. Bobbie waited and, after a moment, Zane slipped his hand in hers. She smiled and rose. "You'll have to tell me about your favorite animals so we can decorate the classroom a little bit more. I was waiting until we met."

Rafi stood there silently, watching as Bobbie and Zain left the room and headed down the hallway.

"Another miracle worker," Malik said.

"This was one of the reasons we hired her," Rafi said. Since he was part of the Department of Education, he had read about Bobbie's career.

"I'm so happy," Catherine said with a hiccup.

Rafi saw the tears in her eyes. "Catherine?"

Catherine waved her hand. "Happy tears. Go ahead. I need to get myself under control before Zain sees me."

Rafi's brother nodded his head and pulled his soon-to-be wife into his arms. Rafi left the room and headed for the classroom. When he got there he stood in the doorway, a smile breaking out on his face.

Zain and Bobbie were sitting at one of the tables, and Zain was drawing an elephant. Bobbie sat there with him quietly talking to him, and Zain was nodding. This woman was good for them. For Zain. For the family. For him.

Bobbie let out a sigh as she and Rafi walked in the garden. The sun was just beginning to set, and the garden was bathed in the orange and yellow hues of the sunset.

"Tired?" Rafi asked.

"Not really. I'm just glad things went so well today with Zain."

"You were worried?" Rafi held her hand as they walked on the mosaic pathway.

"A bit. It's sometimes hard for a child who has suffered a trauma to adjust to a new person." She thought back on the day, about the joy she'd seen on Zain's face as they had drawn pictures and when they had gone down to the stables for a bit. "This may be a bit presumptuous of me since I just met Zain today, but have Catherine and Malik thought about bringing in a child psychologist to check on Zain?"

"You are his teacher, so you are free to ask anything you like. And yes, they have thought about it, but Hassan asked they give Zain a little more time. Compared to when he was first found to now, there is a very big difference."

"I can understand that. Zain needs to get comfortable with being a part of a family once again, one that he feels safe with."

"Yes."

They walked in silence for a few minutes. Bobbie thought about all the things she could do to help Zain feel safe and secure. When Rafi pulled her to a stop, she looked up at him. "Are you ready to play tonight?" he asked.

Instant heat flowed through her veins. "Yes, I would like to."

"Good. Let's sit for a minute." He led her over to a marble bench and they sat. "Since this is the first time we've played together, I want to go over a few things."

"All right."

"Do you remember your safewords?"

"Yes. Bronco to stop and harness to slow down."

Rafi nodded, then his dark eyes turned serious. "I would like to restrain you tonight and use some toys on you."

Bobbie's heart sped up. They were really going to do

this. She nodded. Rafi cupped her chin and raised her face to his.

"Words, sweetheart. I need to hear the words that you're on the same page with me."

"I'm fine with what you want to do tonight."

"While you play tonight, I want to hear your voice, your moans, your passion. You don't need to be silent."

"Okay." Excitement flowed through her body. She was going to do this with Rafi.

"Good. When we get upstairs, I want you to go to your room, undress, and lie down on your bed. I'll be there shortly."

"All right." There was a slight tremor in her voice.

Rafi brushed his lips over hers. "I sense you're nervous."

"A little. It's been a while for me." Bobbie looked down at her hands as they tangled in her lap. None of her boyfriends had caused this level of excitement that coursed through her body right now.

"For me as well, but I will go slow, and you can stop me anytime if you become frightened."

She took a deep breath, glanced up at Rafi, and asked, "How far are we going to go tonight?"

"What do you mean?" His brow wrinkled in thought.

Bobbie looked around. "Are we going to have sex?" she asked in a quiet voice.

A grin played around his lips. "Only if you want." He leaned closer to her. "We can play without sex.

When the time is right. You can tell me when you're ready."

He neatly put the ball back in her court, and she hadn't expected that. "Most men would—"

Rafi shook his head and stopped her words with a light kiss. "I'm not most men. Play is exciting, satisfying and erotic for me."

She nodded. "I think I understand."

"You will." He dropped another kiss against her lips. "Let's go." He drew her to her feet and together they walked back to the palace. He released her when they got to her room. "I'll be back in fifteen minutes."

"Okay." Bobbie slipped into her bedroom and leaned against the closed door. Was she really going to do this? Hell, yes. She pushed away from the door and walked through the bedroom to her bathroom. Fifteen minutes wasn't a lot of time.

She stripped off her clothes, piled her hair on top of her head, and jumped into the shower, quickly cleaning up and shaving. Once done, she dried off, then put her robe on before going back into her bedroom.

Bobbie stopped short when she saw Rafi standing by the side of her bed. He was wearing a pair of black pants and was bare chested. Her mouth watered at all that golden skin. "Ummm." She couldn't find her words. Then he flashed her one of his sexy, bad-boy grins.

"I'm early. I wanted to get prepared." He gestured to the nightstand. "I put your book in the drawer."

She nodded, still unable to do more than stare at his body. Damn, the man was built. When he'd held her, she'd realized he was built, but now ... without thought she crossed the room and ran her finger down the center of his chest.

"Bobbie," he whispered.

"I'm sorry." She snatched her hand back. Hadn't she read somewhere you shouldn't touch your dominant unless he told you to?

"No." He captured her hand and placed it back on his body. "You can touch me all you want, unless I tell you not to."

He released her hand, and she trailed her fingers over his flat brown nipples, down his six-pack abs, to the top of his black pants. Her own skin tingled against his. Could she be so bold?

Her fingers toyed with the elastic on his pants, then his hand captured hers. "No, sweetheart. That is for much later." He brought her hand to his lips and kissed each fingertip. "Now, take off the robe and climb onto the bed."

His husky tone sent shivers of anticipation through her bloodstream. Bobbie stepped away from him, turned her back, took her robe off, and then climbed onto the bed, face down.

Rafi's chuckle reached her ears. "On your back, sweetheart."

Bobbie rolled over and closed her eyes. Would he think

her breasts were too big? She always thought they were. Was she skinny enough? Where was all this insecurity coming from? She was aware of her flaws.

"Beautiful." The word reached her ears before the mattress dipped. "Open your eyes, sweetheart."

She forced her lids up to see Rafi leaning over her, his dark eyes ablaze with desire. Her hands fisted into the bedspread so as not to cover herself.

"Easy," he said, as his hand rested over her fist. "You have a gorgeous body."

Bobbie swallowed. "Really?"

"Yes." He lifted his hand and traced a finger down her nose, over her lips, then down her chest to her belly button. "Your nipples are a dusky rose and already hard, anticipating my touch."

She glanced down and noticed he was right. Her nipples were hard. Her body was reacting to him.

"Now, on some play nights I won't tell you what I'm going to do, but tonight I will. Remember your safewords and relax."

"Easy for you to say," she said. Her body was already on fire.

Rafi looked down at her. "Bobbie, if you don't want to do this ... " He started to move away.

"No." She sat up so fast she almost clipped his chin with her head. "Sorry. I'm just nervous. As I said, it's been a while for me."

Rafi blew out a breath. "I understand. Let's see if I

can put you at ease a little bit more. Can you put your hands over your head and hold them there?" Bobbie lay back and did as he asked. "Good. Now, all I'm going to do is run my fingers over your body. So close your eyes and feel."

Bobbie allowed her lashes to fall. Rafi's touch was feather light, running over her arms and legs. Her toes wiggled as he played with them before he moved back up her body. She held her breath as he circled her breasts then let it out and allowed her body to go lax.

"Good, sweetheart. Just relax." His fingers drew smaller and smaller circles until he brushed one nipple briefly before switching to the other breast.

His touch was so gentle, so soft, her body sank onto the mattress in relaxed bliss. Her legs parted slightly.

"Very good," he whispered, his mouth close to her ear. "I'm glad your hair is up, because I can do this." The pins that held her hair in place were pulled out, but because of the way she lay, her hair fanned out behind her on the pillow. "So beautiful."

The mattress shifted, but Bobbie didn't open her eyes. "Now, I'm going to wrap a scarf around your wrists." Soft fabric encased her wrists as he spoke, then she felt a slight tug. "Okay?" he asked as he ran his fingers between the scarf and her skin.

"Yes," she whispered. She gave an experimental tug and realized he'd tied the scarf to the headboard. She couldn't lower her arms. Her stomach tightened and moisture began to gather between her thighs.

"Oh, yes, you like that." His lips brushed over her forehead before lifting, and then his mouth enveloped her left breast.

"Rafi," she cried out at his hot, wet mouth around her sensitive breast. His tongue flicked against her hard nipple.

"So sensitive," he said, his breath brushing her skin before he moved his attentions to her other breast.

Bobbie squirmed on the bed as her pussy began to pulse. Her skin felt tight as Rafi licked one nipple and played with the other one. Her body reacted to him. But it was more than that; deep down, something inside her began to uncoil, to stretch out and embrace what he was doing.

He lifted his head, and Bobbie forced her eyes open. When had she shut them? Rafi gazed down at her, his dark eyes filled with passion. "So responsive to my touch, my mouth." His palm slid over her stomach toward her mound. "Open your legs, my pet."

She followed his directions. He traced her pussy lips with gentle fingers, and she bucked against his hand. His touch was cool, but then again she was burning up.

"Rafi." She pulled at the restraints, wanting to put her hands on him.

"Tonight, your pleasure is mine." The mattress shifted as he moved between her legs, his shoulders forcing her legs apart. Before she could think to protest, his fingers parted her pussy, and he bent his head.

He licked her, and she bucked against his mouth. Oh, my goodness. Her breath whooshed out of her. None of her boyfriends had ever gone down on her. Well, one had tried, but it had been nothing like this.

Rafi licked and used his tongue to toy with her clit. Electric pulses shot from her pussy to her nipples and back again.

"You taste of honey," Rafi's breath teased her inner thighs.

"I ... " Bobbie couldn't catch her breath as he bent his head again, but this time he sucked her clit between his lips.

"Fuck." The word escaped her lips as her body bucked. Rafi didn't let up; instead, he alternated between licking her and sucking her clit. Her core tightened, then relaxed, then tightened again.

Heat coiled in her pelvis. Her mouth was open as she tried to suck in some breaths, but she couldn't. The sensations Rafi was creating in her body—she'd never felt so many different things at once. Her body quivered.

"That's it," Rafi murmured. "Come for me, my pet. Let me see you explode."

Before Bobbie could respond, the spring coiling inside her broke, and her climax shot through her. She thrashed on the mattress, fighting to get her arms loose, all while sounds of pleasure were slipping from her lips.

Her climax subsided. When she collapsed against the sheets, they felt cool against her back. Rafi crawled up from between her legs, pressing kisses all the way up her body.

"That was ... " She shook her head. "Fantastic doesn't seem to cover it."

He grinned. "You are so sexy when you climax, those wonderful little mewing sounds you make."

Her eyes widened, and she bit her lip. Rafi's grin grew bigger. He leaned down and brushed his lips over hers.

"Such a rich, ripe lip, don't bite it." The second she released her lip, his mouth covered hers.

She could taste her musky flavor on his tongue and lips. Her legs moved against the sheets. Her body was responding to his closeness. And she wanted more. More kinkiness, more Rafi.

Rafi lifted his head from the kiss to stare into Bobbie's languid hazel eyes. She was so responsive to him. She'd mentioned other boyfriends, but said they really hadn't done anything for her. He was proud he could make her climax with just his lips and tongue.

He wanted to do so much more, but one glance at the clock on the nightstand told him it would have to wait. He lifted his hands and undid the scarves around her wrists, then frowned when he saw the reddened skin.

"Bobbie, do you hurt?" He rolled off her and helped her sit up, taking her wrists and rubbing them.

"I'm fine." She glanced down. "Oh. I must have pulled too hard."

He frowned. "Still, I will need to be careful with your fair skin."

"Rafi." She reached up with her free hand and cupped his cheek. "I'm not hurt, they don't hurt at all. I wouldn't lie to you."

He turned his head and kissed her palm. "Very well." He released her wrist, instead slipping his arms around her waist, holding her to him. He didn't like seeing those marks even if they were unintended.

"Now what?" she asked, as he held her.

"Now we rest."

"And?"

"We shall see." Rafi placed the scarves on the nightstand, then looked at Bobbie. "Will it bother you if I remove my pants?"

Her cheeks turned pink. "No." She slid over so there was room for him on the bed.

Rafi removed his pants and laid them on the chair before turning off the light and climbing onto the mattress. Once his eyes adjusted to the darkness, he reached over and pulled her against his chest.

Bobbie's breath brushed over his chest, her breathing rapid. "Relax," he said.

She nodded. Rafi kept his hold on her light, letting her know she was safe and secure.

"Rafi?"

"Yes."

"Are we going to play more tonight?"

The question surprised him. While she'd told him she wasn't very experienced in kink, he hadn't expected this. "You need time to recover."

"But what about you?"

"Me what?"

"You ... " Her hand moved from where it rested on his chest to the base of his cock. "You didn't come."

Rafi inhaled sharply at her soft touch. "I'm fine." He encircled her wrist with his fingers before he glanced down at her.

"But ... " She sank her teeth into her lower lip once again. "I want to please you too."

"I know, but it is not necessary." She started to frown. "Tonight," he added. "Go to sleep, and tomorrow we will play more."

"Very well." Her fingers released his shaft, and Rafi sighed in relief. He didn't mind the discomfort of having a hard-on. Bobbie's satisfaction would always come first for him.

Within a few minutes, Bobbie relaxed and fell asleep. Rafi lay there enjoying the feeling of her in his arms and planning out their next play session.

Three days later, Rafi slipped into the stables with Shadow just as dawn broke. "Good job tonight, Shadow." Rafi stroked the horse as he took off the saddle and put it away. They'd followed a group of Kalif's men further than he had intended. But the good thing was he now knew where some of them were hiding out.

Rafi stifled a yawn as he brushed down Shadow. Then he made sure the horse had food and water before he stripped off the black robe and headdress. He didn't want anyone catching him wearing it.

He walked out of the stables and toward the palace. Maybe he could catch a quick catnap before breakfast. Inside his room, he hid the black clothing, and then fell onto the bed. Yes, a quick nap.

Bobbie smiled as Zain worked on the math problems she'd given him. The last few days had been busy with Zain in the classroom and Rafi in her bedroom. A shiver of anticipation slid over her body.

Rafi had slipped out of her room last night with a whispered kiss. Bobbie wondered why he'd left. He'd been spending the nights with her. Her insides heated.

Yes, they'd played, but Rafi wouldn't let her bring him to completion. She didn't like that. Oh, he brought her to climax, sometimes more than once. Her body was like a finely tuned instrument just for him.

They hadn't made love yet. She was determined to change that, and soon. She wanted to feel him inside her. Bobbie glanced at the clock on the wall. It was almost lunch time. After lunch, she'd take Zain down to the stables. He loved being around the horses, and so did she. It wasn't until she'd started spending more time around the horses that she realized how much she'd missed it. Plus Rafi had promised Zain a riding lesson.

Zain knocked on the table, one of the ways he let her know he was finished with his work. So far, she hadn't gotten the little boy to talk, but it would come. They communicated in other ways.

Bobbie sat down next to Zain and looked at his paper. He had them all right. "Good job." She ruffled his dark hair. "What do you say we get lunch and then spend the afternoon down at the stables?"

Zain nodded, then smiled before jumping up and running out of the room. Bobbie smiled as she put his papers away, then followed.

An hour later, they walked hand in hand down to the stable with Hamaz by their side. Bobbie didn't understand why Rafi felt the need for her to have a bodyguard, but she shrugged it away.

Rafi was in the stable with Ransom, the horse he'd chosen for Zain to ride. Zain started to run, but Rafi shook his head and Zain skidded to a stop.

"Remember, Zain, you don't want to startle Ransom by running."

Zain nodded, then walked cautiously toward the horse. Once Zain was close, he held out his hand so the horse could smell him, then he began petting the horse. Bobbie still wasn't sure about having Zain ride a full-grown Arabian, but Rafi told her Zain was perfectly safe.

"Razan is going to give you your lesson today," Rafi said, holding Zain's hand while leading the horse out of the stables through a side door to the ring.

Bobbie held back and watched. Zain hung on every word Rafi told him. There was a connection there. It was heartwarming to see. Rafi left Zain with Razan after ruffling the boy's hair and walked back to her.

"Why aren't you teaching him today?" she asked.

"One of my mares is having some issues." He took her hand in his. "Come with me while I check in on her?"

She hesitated. "I really should stay here and keep an eye on Zain."

"He's fine." Rafi tugged her close. "Razan is with him and so is Hamaz."

Bobbie looked out at the ring. Rafi was right. Razan was right next to Zain and the horse, with Hamaz standing off to the side watching. "Okay."

Rafi grinned, then led her from the stables to a smaller barn she hadn't noticed before. He drew her inside the cool building. Before she could look around, Rafi pulled her into his arms, and his lips closed over hers.

Unable to help herself, Bobbie wrapped her arms around Rafi's neck and opened her mouth to his. Their tongues touched, tangled, and played with each other. When Rafi gripped the back of her neck, her knees grew weak, and she clung to him until he broke the kiss.

"So beautiful," he whispered.

"You make my bones melt," she told him.

"And you make me hard."

Her body caught fire at his words, then the whinny of a horse caught her attention. The horse's head appeared over the stall door. "We're being watched."

"What?" Rafi's stiffened, then relaxed when he saw the mare. "That's Jewel." He guided Bobbie over to the stall door.

"Hello, Jewel," Bobbie greeted the horse. "You said she was having issues."

"Yeah, with her due date in another week, she's been really grouchy."

Bobbie laughed. "Well, you try carrying a baby around for months." She rubbed the horse's nose, but noticed the horse's eyes were glassy. "Is she having allergy issues?"

"She's had some light clear discharge from her eyes; we've been treating it." Rafi moved up next to Bobbie. "But it keeps coming back."

"Can I open the stall door?"

"Sure." Rafi stood back, and she unlocked the door and pulled it open.

Bobbie let out a gasp. "Rafi, go call your vet, now."

He didn't hesitate; he turned and sprinted out of the barn. "It's okay, girl," Bobbie crooned. She moved carefully, keeping one hand on the mare's neck, stroking as she ran her hand over Jewel's belly.

Rafi ran back into the barn. He wasn't even out of breath. "Vet will be here in ten minutes. I couldn't tell him why you had me call him."

"Because Jewel here has her uterus twisted." She kept rubbing the mare's extended belly.

"How did you know that?" Rafi asked.

"I've seen it before. I don't think it's been going on for more than a day. Has she been eating okay?"

"Yes, but ... I noticed she seemed to be in pain; we thought it was her allergies, as she's always had them."

"You gave her painkillers?"

"Yes, mild ones. She seemed fine."

"When?"

"Yesterday, but now—" His word were interrupted by a loud gurgling sound.

"We can confirm for sure when the vet gets here, but that's another sign." Bobbie kept rubbing the horse. "It will be okay, girl."

When the vet arrived, Bobbie backed out of the stall and let him work, but she watched. Rafi stood beside her, his body stiff. "It's going to be okay," she said, as the vet and his tech finally got Jewel into a roll position and began to maneuver her.

"Very good," the vet said as he and his tech helped Jewel back to her feet. The mare let out a whinny and then went over and drank water.

"It is a good thing you called," the vet said to Rafi. "She had minor twisting, but if you hadn't noticed, it could have been worse."

"I didn't notice, Bobbie did," Rafi said, pointing to her.

The vet looked at her, then his eyes crinkled at the edges. "And how did you know the horse was under distress?"

Bobbie smiled. "I'm a qualified vet tech, and I've been around horses most of my life. When I saw her stomach and her movements, I had suspicions, but when I touched her belly, I could tell."

The vet nodded. "Keep her around, Rafi." Then the vet and his tech left the barn.

"Vet tech?" He drew her into his arms and stared down at her.

"Yes, I wasn't able to use the degree unless I worked at a veterinarian's office, and in Seattle that meant dogs, cats, and other small animals. I wanted horses, but it wasn't meant to be. That's why I also got my teaching degree."

"You have hidden talents."

"You have no idea," she whispered.

Rafi slipped into Bobbie's room that night with his play bag. He'd finally gotten his order of silk rope that wouldn't leave marks on her fair skin.

"Bobbie," he called out.

"Bedroom."

He crossed the room and stopped just inside the doorway. Bobbie was lying on her bed in a sheer nightgown with a big smile on her face.

"I see you're eager to get started." His heart raced. He loved how open she was with him. He set his bag on the chair and stripped down to his shorts. Then he opened his bag and pulled out the rope.

Her eyes widened when he knelt on the mattress. "This rope shouldn't leave marks on your skin." He stroked her right arm before lifting it over her head, then did the same with the left. "Keep them there."

Rafi shook out a soft cloth and then the rope. He wound the cloth over her wrists, then looped the rope and tied it to the headboard.

"Okay?" he asked.

"Yes." Her voice was soft, and her breathing had already increased.

"If your arms start to fall asleep, tell me."

"Of course."

He moved to the end of the bed and did the same with her ankles, except those he pulled apart, so she was open to him.

Rafi climbed off the mattress. He took out a pair of safety scissors and set them on the nightstand, then pulled out his toys. Rafi glanced over at Bobbie to see her watching him with wide eyes.

"I should have taken off your nightgown before I tied you up," he said.

She blew out a breath. "There are ties; just undo them, and you can slip it off."

His eyebrows rose. He leaned over, found the ties, and released them. "Clever," he said, as he removed the fabric from her. "And when did you buy this naughty piece of lingerie?"

Her cheeks turned pink. "I ordered it from the UK," she said softly.

Rafi grinned and tossed the gown on the chair. He

picked up his nipple toy and concealed it, then he climbed onto the bed again. "Safewords?"

"Harness and bronco."

"Good." Rafi leaned over her, then rained kisses over her face and lower until he came to her breast. Already her nipples were hard and begging for attention. He covered her right breast with his hand, massaging it and then rolling her nipple between his thumb and forefinger.

"That feels so good," Bobbie said.

"It will get better." He lowered his mouth to her other breast, and Bobbie moaned as he licked and sucked, then he switched. Once her nipples were wet and straining, he pulled out his toy.

"What is that?" she asked with a little tremble in her voice.

"A very fun toy." Rafi slipped the cups over her nipples, assuring there was a good seal before squeezing the bulb.

"Ahhhh." Bobbie's neck arched, and she pulled against the ropes restraining her.

"Like that." Rafi chuckled and kissed his way down to her mound. He went lower. Her pussy was wet and her clit begging for attention. He took the last cylinder and placed it over her clit. Once there was a seal he waited until her body relaxed against the bed before he squeezed the bulb in his hand.

She stiffened, then cried out as he squeezed the bulb again. "Rafi," she called his name.

"What are you feeling, my love?"

"I ..." Her breathing was erratic, and her skin flushed. "It's amazing and scary at the same time."

"Oh." He squeezed the bulb again a few times in rapid succession.

"It's like there's a pair of mouths on my tits and one on my clit." She started squirming against the sheets.

"Good, that's how it's suppose to feel." He squeezed the blub again and again until Bobbie couldn't stop moving on the bed. Time to take it up another notch.

He reached over and grabbed the vibrator. He traced her pussy lips with the tip of the toy, coating it with her juices, then slipped it into her pussy.

Bobbie opened her mouth and yanked at the restraints as he pushed in, but especially when he pulled it out, because he would squeeze the blub in his hand, causing the nipple and clit suckers to tighten.

The flushing of her body turned a darker red as she squirmed. Once the vibrator was seated fully in her pussy, he turned it on.

"Rafi," she cried out his name. "I'm going to come."

"Come for me, baby," he whispered, keeping one hand on the vibrator and the other squeezing the blub. "Let me see you fall apart."

Her head thrashed against the pillow as he continued to take her higher and higher. Just as she was about to break, Rafi leaned over and captured her lips with his.

She screamed into his mouth as her orgasm took over. Her entire body shook as they kissed. When Rafi lifted his head, they were both panting. With care, he reached down, turned the vibrator off, and pulled it from her body.

He waited until the tremors running through her body stopped, then he removed the suckers from her clit and nipples. There were little red rings around her nipples, but those would fade.

Rafi tossed the toys into his bag, then began to untie Bobbie. He rubbed her legs after he released them, and then her arms.

"Okay?" he asked quietly after he put the rope away.

"Oh, yes." Her lashes rose and she gazed at him. "Someone has some very naughty toys."

"You enjoyed them." He ran his finger down her nose.

"Yes, but now it's time for you."

"Me?"

Bobbie sat up with a gleam in her eyes. "Lie down."

Rafi was surprised at her commanding tone, but indulged her. He laid down on his back as she scooted to the side of the bed.

"Time for me to make you feel good." She slipped her fingers under his shorts and pulled them down. He lifted his hips so she could slip them over his ass and off his legs. His cock was hard.

"Someone needs attention." She trailed her fingers up his legs and over his shaft, and before he could guess her intention, her fingers encircled the base, and her mouth enveloped the head.

Rafi's fingers curled into his palms to stop from reaching for her. She licked and sucked his dick.

"You taste so good, all male," she said when she lifted her head.

"Bobbie, you don't have to do this," he said, and she didn't.

"I want to. You pleasure me more than I pleasure you. Tonight, I want you to enjoy." She lowered her head again.

Up and down her mouth went, her tongue tasting him as well. The sensations from her sucking went through his cock all the way to his balls, and then through the rest of his body.

His nerves tingled with anticipation as she stroked him with each dip of her head. Bobbie never hesitated, but kept going. His balls tightened and his spine tingled.

"Baby, I'm going to come soon."

His words didn't have the effect he thought they would. Instead of lifting her head and finishing him off with her hand, she re-doubled her efforts, sucking even harder and faster.

Rafi raised his hands and tangled in her hair with the intention of pulling her away, but she resisted him, and her free hand cupped his balls.

He let out a moan as she rolled his balls in her hand, and he started spurting into her mouth. She hummed against his cock, and he couldn't hold back his orgasm any more. He clamped his lips together to stop from shouting out as he came into her mouth.

Spurt and spurt, his body taunt until he was finished, then he collapsed against the mattress. Instead of lifting her head, Bobbie lapped around his cock before she rose up and kissed the head of his dick.

"Damn, woman," he said. "Your mouth should be registered as a lethal weapon."

"Just remember that." She smiled at him and began to climb off the bed.

"Where are you going?" he asked.

"Bathroom, be right back."

Rafi smiled as he rearranged himself and waited for Bobbie to return. When she returned with a washcloth in her hand, she knelt on the bed and cleaned up his cock and balls before throwing the cloth back into the bathroom.

When she climbed back into the bed, he snagged her into his arms. "You are a wonderful woman," he said.

"You're not half bad yourself." She snuggled against him, her lashes already closing.

Rafi shook his head. She was worn out. Then he yawned. So was he.

Three weeks later, Rafi held the reins for Mercury and Charmer as Razan held Tzar and Orion. The horses were not happy, but they were allowing the wedding decorations to be draped over them in preparation.

Khalid wanted to nix the open-air carriage being pulled by horses from the royal stable that would take the bride to the church and then the bride and groom back to the palace. But Malik told Khalid it was tradition, and he wasn't going to deny the people.

Rafi didn't blame Khalid for his unease. Rafi had been trying to help his brother as much as possible. With the wedding reception at the palace, Khalid had insisted on full background checks on everyone who would be working in the palace that day. All the help were local, but Rafi had spent his night with his brother, reading through the checks.

And the security ... Rafi let out a breath. There was more security now than ever. Again, he couldn't fault his brother for his caution, but it hindered Rafi from being able to sneak out at night and see what Kalif was up to.

He'd only made one trip in the last two weeks, and that one was a bust. But maybe that was a good thing. Maybe Kalif was keeping a low profile. The horses shifted in his hold. "It's okay," he crooned to them.

"Can you walk them around, please?" the groomer asked as he finished up.

Rafi nodded. Razan and he walked the horses around, ensuring the fabric didn't interfere with their gait. "Very good," the groomer said. "It will take about an hour to get them ready."

"Very well," Rafi said. As soon as the groomer was through, Rafi led the horses over to the pasture and let them out. He'd let them run a bit. Tomorrow was going to be a long day for all of them.

He glanced up and saw Bobbie and Zain walking toward the ring. A smile flittered over his lips as he crossed the ring to them.

"My two favorite people." He hopped over the fence. He curled his hand behind Bobbie's neck and gave her a quick kiss before ruffling Zain's hair.

Zain pointed to Ransom's stall.

Rafi looked at Samir, who nodded. "Sure. Samir will be with you." He watched the two head for the stables. "How are you today, my beautiful lady?" Rafi pulled her into his embrace.

"Fine. What were you doing with the horses?" Her voice was a little breathless.

"Making sure everything is ready for tomorrow." He guided her away from the ring. Hamaz followed but gave them plenty of space. "The horses will draw the carriage Catherine will ride in to the church, then bring both Malik and Catherine back to the palace."

"Sounds like a fairy tale." She remembered pictures from the royal wedding in England. "I noticed the colors. Very beautiful."

"The royal colors." He drew her to stop underneath one of the large trees that graced the property. "Once this wedding is over with, we'll have more time together." He laid his palm on her cheek.

"Rafi, it's okay." She tilted her head into his touch. "We've all been busy."

"Yes, but I miss you." He wanted nothing more than to sweep her into his arms, carry her up to her bedroom, and have an impromptu play session. But he couldn't; he had responsibilities.

"I miss you too," she whispered. "How long is all the security going to be an issue?" She glanced over at Hamaz.

"A while, I'm afraid. Once the wedding is done and all the guests are gone, it will get a little better. Is Hamaz bothering you?" While Rafi trusted Khalid to hire only the best, men could be bought off.

"No. It's just a bit disconcerting to have a shadow when I'm walking around the gardens."

"It will be better soon." Once the wedding was done he could continue his nightly activities and maybe find out where Kalif was and what his plans were.

"I shouldn't complain."

Rafi pulled her into his arms, enjoying the feel of her against his body. Her arms encircled him. "You're not used to it."

Childish laughter had them both turning toward the ring. Zain was on Ransom's back trying to urge the horse to go faster. Samir stood nearby.

"He laughed," Rafi said.

"Yes." Bobbie leaned her head against Rafi's shoulder. "I'm not exactly sure what is happening, but I have some ideas."

"Tell me." He wanted to know what she was thinking.

"He's become more comfortable with me and being in the palace. I think he's starting to remember."

"Hassan said it was the mind protecting Zain."

"Right. Traumatic events will do that."

He tightened his hold on her, and she squeezed him back.

"He's seven. But I'm hoping now that he's more comfortable, he'll start talking to me. But there is something else, and I've been able to confirm it over the last few weeks."

"What is that?" He turned so he could see her face.

"Zain is very intelligent. I've been giving him fourth-grade math problems and reading comprehension tests. He's acing them."

Rafi glanced from her to the happy boy riding around the ring. "He's always seemed to be bright."

"Yes." She rubbed her forehead.

"Are you worried?" She had no reason to be, as far as he was concerned.

"A little bit. Rafi, I don't know anything about his parents. Do you know how he was taught before now?"

"I don't, but we can ask Malik or Catherine."

"That will work, but not until later. Let them enjoy their wedding and honeymoon."

Rafi smiled and held her close as they watched Zain on the horse.

Bobbie climbed out of bed and stretched. Today was Catherine's and Malik's wedding day. She'd probably watch it on the TV and just lie around, maybe read a book or two. It was a family event and she wasn't family, not matter how much Rafi might think she was.

She was sipping the coffee she'd made in her room when someone knocked. Bobbie stood, made sure her robe was belted tightly, and opened the door. A young lady stood there with a box in her hand.

"Lady Bobbie," she said. "If I may please come in?"

Bobbie stepped back and allowed the woman in. She shut the door and leaned against it. "What can I do for you?"

"Nothing. I am Tahira, and I am here to help you get ready."

"Ready for what?" She frowned.

"The wedding, of course. Prince Rafi gave me instructions, and we don't have a lot of time." Tahira swept into the bedroom.

Wedding? "Now, wait a second." Bobbie went into her bedroom to see Tahira standing by the bed.

"Please, Lady Bobbie, if you would take a quick shower, I will lay everything out so I can help you."

"Tahira," Bobbie said, "I didn't plan on going to the wedding."

"Prince Rafi said you are coming. Please, Lady Bobbie, there is a lot to do." Tahira patted her pocket, then scrunched up her nose. "I forgot." Tahira pulled a folded piece of paper from her pocket and handed it to Bobbie.

She opened the paper and read the note.

Sweetheart, I know you didn't think any of us were serious when we said you would be my date at the wedding, but we were. I have sent Tahira with a gown for you to wear, plus she will help you with your makeup and hair. Malik and Catherine want you at their wedding as one of their honored guests. It wasn't until this morning Catherine realized she didn't issue you a formal invitation, and I told her I would take care of it. So this is it. I'll be waiting to escort you to the church. Don't be late. P.S. If you're late, I will punish you in the most delicious fashion tonight.

The note shook in her hand. Oh, my goodness, she'd never expected ... she shook her head. "Please Tahira, would you find Prince Rafi and tell him I appreciate the effort, but I can't attend the wedding." It didn't feel right to her. She was just Zain's teacher, and technically she was dating a prince. She shook her head.

"I have my orders, Lady Bobbie. Prince Rafi is to be obeyed." Then she pulled out a second piece of paper and handed it to Bobbie.

Bobbie, this is just a quick note to tell you I want you at my wedding. Rafi said you would refuse, but I'm hoping you won't. I need all the friendly faces I can get. So please do me this favor and come. Catherine. P.S. Zain is so excited you will be there to see him as ring bearer.

Aw, hell. Catherine knew just how to get to her. Folding the two notes, Bobbie slipped them into the nightstand drawer, then looked at Tahira. "Okay, I guess I'm in your hands."

"Excellent." Tahira clapped her hands. "Shower, then I will start with your hair."

An hour later, Bobbie stared at herself in the mirror. Tahira had taken her dark hair and somehow piled it high on her head with red, gold, and white ribbons. Her makeup was subtle and made her hazel eye color sparkle.

"Tahira, you are a miracle worker," Bobbie said.

Tahira waved her hand. "You have beautiful silky hair, Lady Bobbie. Come, I will help you put on your dress so it doesn't ruin your makeup."

Bobbie stood up and turned. Tahira was holding a beautiful white gown in her arms. But it was more than that. The gown had red and gold entwined into the fabric along with gold embellishments that looked like the head of a fox.

"Please hold still," Tahira said, as she lifted her arms. Bobbie waited, and when directed, slid her arms into the sleeves. The dress fell around her body.

The fabric was light, yet silky. Bobbie took a deep breath and turned toward the full-length mirror on the closet door. Her breath caught in her throat.

The dress hugged her curves but flattered them at the

same time. She barely recognized herself. She looked like a fairytale princess.

"Now for the shoes." Tahira held out a pair of white ballet flats. Bobbie took them and slid them on. Everything fit perfectly.

"Beautiful. Now come, it is almost time." Tahira took her hand and led her out of the bedroom. The guards all stood at attention as they walked by, and Bobbie wondered why they did that. They never had before. Maybe it was a wedding thing.

They came to a halt in the foyer. "Prince Rafi will be here in a minute," Tahira said, then she ran off.

Bobbie shook her head, then movement caught her eye. And her mouth dropped open. Rafi strode into the room. His robe was white with red and gold woven through the fabric in subtle stripes. He also wore a sash with the same colors. Metals decorated the right side of the robe, and he wore a sword on his left side.

"You are exquisite," he said in a soft voice.

"You're not bad yourself." She swallowed, her throat was dry. The way he looked at her ... she couldn't explain it except to say she felt like a piece of chocolate cake he wanted to devour.

"I am honored to be your escort today." He gave her a bow.

"Rafi," she started, but he shook his head.

"No arguments. We are going to a wedding." He drew her hand through his and led her out the front door. One of the black SUVs was waiting for them, with Hamaz holding the door.

Hamaz was dressed in a black uniform with a red-and-gold sash. "Thank you, Hamaz," she said, as Rafi helped her into the vehicle. Once she was settled, he closed the door, rounded the vehicle, and climbed in beside her.

Hamaz sat in the front seat along with the driver. The driver wore the same uniform as Hamaz. "Formal uniforms?" she asked.

"Yes." Rafi turned to her. "We only use them on very special occasions, and a royal wedding is one of them."

"I see; then why am I in the same colors?" She'd wondered about that when she'd first seen him. The answer dawned on her. "I'm dressed in royal colors, aren't I?"

Rafi reached over and took her hand in his. "Yes, you are my date for the wedding, and you are beautiful."

"But ... " She shook her head. "Why? I'm just Zain's teacher."

"You're so much more than that to me." He raised her hand to his lips and kissed the back of it. "Why not show everyone that you're mine?"

Bobbie swallowed. His declaration filled her heart with excitement. If any other man had said that to her, she would be protesting, but Rafi treated her with the utmost respect in and out of the bedroom.

"That may be, but won't my being in the royal colors draw speculation?"

"Sara is wearing the same colors."

"Sara is engaged to Hassan." The SUV turned, and Bobbie glanced out the front window and froze. "Oh, my." The words slipped from her lips as the vehicle drove down the narrow streets of Bashir City, which were now decorated with the royal colors and bells.

"The people of Bashir are very excited about Malik's and Catherine's wedding," Rafi said. "They did all the decorating of the streets."

"It's so pretty." Bobbie turned in her seat, gazing out the window at the people lining the streets, all waving at the vehicle as it went by. The windows were tinted dark, so Bobbie was pretty sure no one knew exactly who was in the vehicle.

"Our people are becoming the proud people they once were," Rafi said quietly.

She tilted her head as she turned to him. "What do you mean?"

"That's a story for later." He brushed a kiss over her nose. "Today is a celebration, and I don't want to ruin it."

His words made Bobbie frown. How would he ruin the celebration by telling her about the people? She filed her questions away for later. The SUV pulled up in front of a church.

The building was large, with carved pillars and stained-glass windows. The staircase was covered in a red rug, and there were lots of security around. Rafi jumped out, and Bobbie heard the roar of the crowd.

He opened her door and took her hand to help her from the SUV. The crowd went wild cheering as they moved away from the vehicle and walked up the stairs. Khalid stood at the top, dressed the same as Rafi.

"Brother, little sister," Khalid said.

"Little sister?" Bobbie stared at Khalid.

"A pet name," Rafi said quietly.

Khalid's eyebrows rose. "Mom and Dad are just inside the door. You escort Bobbie first, and we'll follow. Once they're seated we can take our places."

"What?" Bobbie's eyes widened.

Rafi didn't say a word. He entwined their arms, and he began leading her through the doors and down the aisle.

The royal colors were draped everywhere, and the place was full. Bobbie swallowed and tried to smile. She kept her gaze straight. Why was Rafi doing this? They were just lovers, that was it. Her nerves danced as they reached the front, and Rafi led her to the empty space in front.

She wanted to protest when Rafi released her arm and motioned for her to sit, but she bit her lip instead and sat down. Rafi threw her a sexy grin before turning to join Malik and Hassan.

Khalid arrived with Jamal and Anna. Anna sat down next to Bobbie and Jamal on the other side of Anna, then Khalid joined his brothers.

Bobbie twisted her hands together. She didn't know

what to expect. When she'd been told she was attending the wedding, she figured she'd be in back, and she could just follow everyone else. But being in front ... she curled her toes in her shoes.

"It's okay, my dear," Anna whispered.

Bobbie turned her head.

"The wedding should be similar to ones you've been to. We accept all religions here in Bashir. The family is mainly Christian, since Jamal's father married a woman from the UK. Our Middle Eastern ancestors will be honored as well."

"Thank you," Bobbie whispered. "I really don't belong here."

"Of course you do." Anna patted her hand where it rested on her lap. "You're part of the royal household."

A group of men with drums came out and everyone stood. Bobbie's heart sped as the men began to play the drums. It was an intense beat with different sounds. Zain in his royal robe walked down the aisle carrying a white pillow, then Sara was behind him, and finally Catherine.

Catherine's dress was a mixture of fabric and lace and included the royal colors. She wore a veil over her face and walked alone. Bobbie wondered if Catherine's father was dead. The beat of the drums flowed through the room, chasing away her thoughts.

When Catherine reached the front, she turned to Malik, who took her hands in his. Everyone sat, and the wedding began.

Five hours later, Rafi pulled Bobbie into his arms for another dance. The wedding had gone off without a hitch. But then he had expected it to. Security had been tight, and everyone was on their guard in case Kalif or his men tried something, but they hadn't.

Now that his duties were finished and the older people retired for the evening, he could dance all he wanted with his lady. She'd been very nervous when he seated her with him at the bridal table, but he wouldn't let her run away.

The reception was a small group of people, mainly people who affected Malik's and Catherine's lives, local government officials, advisors, and friends of the family. They wanted to keep it small for security reasons.

"I noticed Catherine doesn't seem to have any family here," Bobbie said quietly to him as the music started.

"No." Rafi kept his voice low. "Catherine wants nothing to do with her parents." The spectacle they had caused reinforced Catherine's decision to keep them out of her life.

"They're a beautiful couple," Bobbie said as they danced, waving her hand in the direction of Malik and Catherine.

"Yes. I'm glad the wedding is done. It gave the people of Bashir something to enjoy even if it turned the house-hold crazy."

"It was a moving ceremony, a blend of old and new," Bobbie said.

"Yes." He'd been surprised when Catherine had made the suggestion to use the drummers. "Catherine wanted something of Bashir at her wedding. The drummers have performed at ceremonies over the years."

"I wasn't sure what to expect. Your mother explained that all religions are welcome in Bashir, but the family is Christian."

"Yes, my grandfather married a British woman, as my father did and now my brother."

Bobbie let out a sigh.

"Tired?" he asked.

"A bit." She laid her head on his shoulder as they danced. "It's been a long day."

"It has." He glanced around the room. Khalid was already gone, probably checking on security. Malik took Catherine's hand and led her from the room. "Shall we sneak out?"

Bobbie's eyes widened. "Do we dare?"

"Malik and Catherine just left. I think we're safe." He danced them toward the ballroom doors.

"Won't someone miss us?"

"Hassan is in charge of the reception, so he can deal with everyone." They slipped out the doors. Rafi took her hand and led her past the guards and through the palace. They'd been on the public side, where the ballroom was. Now he wanted to get to their private area.

"I never realized how big the palace was," Bobbie said, as he pulled her with him.

"Yes, we have the public area and the private family area. We've been adding on to the private side with Malik and Catherine getting married, and Dad stepping down."

"So that means Catherine is now queen?"

"It does." He guided her to a stop at his room. "Spend the night with me in my room?"

She nodded, and Rafi opened the door and guided her inside. Once he'd closed and locked the door, he swept her into his arms and carried her into his bedroom. He slowly undressed her and placed her on his bed. Time to worship his own queen.

B obbie woke the next morning to see Rafi watching her. "Good morning," she said.

"Morning, beautiful." Rafi lowered his head and took her lips. When he lifted his mouth from her, Bobbie tried to catch her breath. That's what Rafi did to her.

"What's on the agenda today?" she asked.

"Well, since it's Sunday and I doubt anyone is going to be doing much today after the wedding, why don't I go down and get us some breakfast? We can eat here and talk."

"Talk?" She frowned. "What do you want to talk about?"

"About you." He brushed another kiss against her lips, and then climbed out of bed.

Bobbie blew out a breath, when it caught in her throat at the sight of his gorgeous ass. Damn, the man was sexy.

Rafi walked to the closet, pulled out a pair of pants and slipped them on, then grabbed a shirt and laid it over the bottom of the bed. "You can wear that. I'll be back in about ten minutes." He sauntered out of the room.

Bobbie sat staring at the doorway until she heard the outer door shut. She jumped out of bed, grabbed the shirt, and ran into the bathroom. Ten minutes wasn't a long time. She found the pins from her hair last night still sitting on the vanity. She used them to put her hair up and climbed into the shower.

After the quickest shower on record, she dried off, brushed her teeth, and slipped on Rafi's shirt. She sniffed the sleeve. It smelled like him. Leather, horses, and all male. Undoing her hair, she used her fingers to comb it out a bit, and then went back into the bedroom.

She found her panties under the bed, slipped them on, and headed for the sitting room. Rafi opened the door and strode in with a tray. Bobbie hurried over to the door, holding it open for him and then closing it once he was in the room.

The aroma of fresh roasted beans teased her nose. "Coffee." She pounced on the silver pot and poured herself a cup, added cream and sugar, then blew on it before taking a sip. "Ah, the elixir of the gods."

Rafi laughed. "I had a feeling you'd want coffee."

Bobbie sat on the sofa as Rafi began unloading the tray. "I brought a little bit of everything."

Bacon, eggs, sausage, toast, and potatoes filled two large plates. Bobbie's stomach growled. She ducked her head and set her coffee on the table.

"Good, you're hungry," Rafi said, sitting down and handing her a plate along with utensils.

The smells of food made her mouth water. Dinner last night was a long time ago. Laying her napkin over her lap, she cradled the plate in one hand, her fork in the other, and began eating.

"This is so good."

Rafi just smiled at her before they both continued eating. Once her plate was empty she set it down on the table and poured herself more coffee. "That was perfect, thank you." She leaned over and kissed his cheek.

"I'm glad you liked it." Rafi poured himself coffee, then turned so he was facing her. "We really haven't had a lot of alone time."

"We have played, and last night ... " Her body went hot. Last night they'd made love, more than once. Rafi took her to heights no one else ever had.

"Last night we made love," he said. "But I really don't know that much about you."

"You do," she said, not really wanting to have this conversation.

"I know you came from Seattle in the States, a little bit

about your childhood, and why you became a teacher. But I want to know more."

"Like what?" She took a sip of her coffee to ease the knot in her stomach.

"Tell me how you came to know horses."

"My dad ran a horse farm when I was younger." She sat back and allowed herself to think of that happy time.

"He raised thoroughbreds, you mentioned before."

"Yep. Mainly for ranchers and rodeo. I grew up around horses, and I loved them." Montana was a great place to live, and she'd enjoyed life there. She gave him a small smile, and then it faded.

"You were happy, now you're sad. What are you thinking?"

"I told you my father died when I was sixteen."

"Yes." Rafi set his coffee down and then took her cup from her, placing it on the table as well. "How did he die?"

The knot in her stomach grew bigger. "I'd known for a while my parents were not getting along, but I was either in school or helping Dad. Well, I didn't realize how bad things were."

She closed her eyes, only to open them when Rafi slipped his arm around her shoulders, giving her support.

"I came home from school one day, and the police were there. I didn't know what was going on." She remembered the police cars in front of the house, the pitying looks of the officers as she walked into her home. "What I didn't know was my dad had a gambling problem. He was a risk-taker with money. He'd been on a bad streak, and he was trying to make it up. He'd put up the ranch as collateral."

Tears filled her eyes. "It was time to pay up. Men came to the house to collect. My mom called the police because she didn't know what was going on. When they arrived everything came out. So they went to the barn." Her voice cracked.

Rafi lifted her and cradled her on his lap, his arms encircling her, reminding her she was not alone. "My dad killed himself. He couldn't face what he'd done." She sniffled. Even after all this time she was still angry with her dad for risking everything and losing it.

"What happened after that?"

"Well, the men owned the ranch, so Mom and I packed and moved from Montana to a small apartment outside of Seattle."

"Why Seattle?"

"Mom wanted no memories of the ranch or Montana. I finished up high school, and you know the rest. She kicked me out on my eighteenth birthday."

Rafi held her close. Part of her was glad this was out, but another part of her wondered if she was getting in too deep with Rafi.

Hell, who was she kidding? She was falling for him, and that scared her more than anything. She was broken inside, and there was no fixing her.

"What about men in your life?"

Bobbie gave a short laugh. "There have only been two. One in college and one after college. I just couldn't seem to find a man I wanted in my life." She almost gave a bitter laugh. What man wanted a broken woman? A woman who couldn't have children.

"Okay, enough of this depressing subject." She tilted her head up. "What would you like to do today?"

Rafi gazed down at her with those dark eyes of his. "I want to make you feel cherished and loved."

Her heart pounded. "How?"

Rafi grinned, cradled her in his arms, stood, and then strode into the bedroom. "Today you are my queen." He placed her on the bed and continued to show her how much he cherished her.

"Did you and Bobbie have a good day yesterday?" Khalid asked as he walked with Rafi down to the stables the next morning.

"Yes." Rafi hid a smile. After he'd made love to her, they'd had a play session before he'd held her while she napped. After she'd told him about her father, he'd wanted her to feel better. It wasn't her fault her father had risked everything.

"Good. I got one of those mysterious notes again," Khalid said.

Rafi's nerves danced. He hadn't ridden out to investigate since before the wedding, but one of his informants had slipped him some information the night before the wedding. Rafi had finally got around to writing it all down and putting it on Khalid's desk.

If Khalid ever found out it was Rafi giving him the information, and how he was getting it, there would be hell to pay.

"What did it say this time?" Rafi kept his tone neutral.

"Only that Kalif was moving his operation more northeast, and as soon as he'd finished setting it up, I would be informed."

"Well, that's good news, our efforts are working."

"Yes." Khalid sighed. "Soon I think we'll have him cornered, and then we can take down his operation."

His brother's voice was skeptical. "But?"

"I'm not sure I can trust this information."

"I can understand that, but didn't you get a note last month that led to the cache of money and opium in one of the villages?"

"I did, but ..." Khalid shook his head. "I can't figure out how this person is getting into the palace. I've resorted to putting a camera in my office to see if I can figure it out. It has to be someone here on palace grounds. Do we have an ally in Kalif's camp, or is someone setting us up?"

Camera? He'd make sure he knew its position before he placed another note on Khalid's desk. "I can see your point, but so far the person has been on our side." Rafi had to bite his tongue not to reveal he was the source. He had a meeting with his informant next week, and hope-fully they could soon get rid of Kalif and the opium.

Already the drug rehabilitation unit, plus Hassan's and Sara's efforts with the villages, were squeezing Kalif out. Even the other tribal leaders had denounced him, so there was progress.

"Yes," Khalid said as they reached the stables. "You and Bobbie kept a low profile yesterday."

"We did." Rafi went from stall to stall, petting the horses when they stuck their heads out.

"So another one of us bites the dust."

Rafi laughed. "Maybe. Bobbie is like a skittish horse. I have to tread carefully and lightly."

"Because of her background?"

He should have known, Khalid had background checks on everyone. "Yes, and I suspect there is something else she's hiding."

"I can give you the file."

Rafi shook his head. "No. She'll tell me when she's ready."

"Good luck, brother. Malik and Hassan didn't have an easy time of it."

"They didn't." Rafi watched his brother walk away as his stomach knotted. What was the big secret she was keeping? Khalid had only said he'd give him the file, not that he knew what the secret was. Did that mean it wasn't in her file? Possibly something so personal wouldn't show up.

Shadow snorted, and Rafi ran his hand over Shadow's neck. "We'll ride soon."

Bobbie sat at her desk later that afternoon going over Zain's work. She'd had Hamaz take Zain down to the stable so he could ride. She shook her head going over Zain's work.

He was well above second-grade level. She needed to talk to Catherine and Malik about what schooling he'd had up until now. Today, she'd given Zain third-grade work, and he'd flown through it, getting a hundred percent on everything, including the spelling test.

If she was going to keep Zain interested in school, she would need more information. Bobbie stood up, stretched, and then went over to the bookcase. She pulled out a book for fourth graders. Tomorrow she'd give Zain a few lessons from this book and see what happened.

"Bobbie," Rafi's husky voice floated into the classroom, and Bobbie lifted her head from the papers on her desk.

"Hi." Her blood heated. Yesterday had been a magical day in her book. They'd talked, made love, played, and then made love again. She was getting in way too deep with Rafi but couldn't seem to stop herself.

"Do you realize dinner is in fifteen minutes?" He stepped into the room.

"What?" She glanced at the clock on the wall, surprised to see it was six forty-five. "I didn't realize it was so late." She stood. "Oh, lord, I sat too long." Bobbie put her hands on her back and stretched.

"Bad girl," Rafi said, walking over to her. He put his hands on her shoulders and rubbed.

"That feels so good." She let her head fall forward as he massaged her shoulders.

"What has you staying so late in the classroom?" he asked.

"I was getting some lessons ready for Zain tomorrow."

"I thought you had stuff for him already."

"I did." Bobbie placed her hands over his on her shoulders, stopping his massage. "I need to talk with Malik. Zain's work is above that of a second grader."

Rafi turned her to face him. "Come on, let's get to dinner, and then you can talk with Malik."

"Okay."

Bobbie sat down in a chair in Malik's office after dinner and Rafi sat next to her, while Catherine sat on a stool next to her husband. The gold band gleamed on her finger.

"You wanted to talk about Zain," Malik said.

"Yes. Can you tell me what type of schooling he had before I began teaching him?"

Catherine frowned. "Is he failing?" she asked quietly.

"Oh, no." Bobbie sat forward. "I didn't mean that. He's doing excellent work."

Malik took his wife's hand. "When I talked to the neighbors and the local school, they said Zain never attended. It's possible his mother or father taught him. I honestly don't know much about the family." Malik shook his head.

"Honey," Catherine said, "we've discussed this. There is no way anyone can keep up with every family in Bashir."

"I know," Malik said, giving his wife a smile.

"Well, if that's the case, and we don't know, I'll keep proceeding the way I am." Bobbie held up her hand when Catherine started to speak. "Zain is doing beyond second-grade work. I gave him third-grade work today, and he aced it all. Tomorrow I'll give him some fourth-grade work and see what happens."

"Are you okay teaching at these levels?" Malik asked.

"I am. I have my degree through sixth grade so I'm good." Zain was going to be a challenge, but she'd rise to it. She loved teaching and learning.

"Good. Go with your gut with Zain, and we'll go from there," Malik said.

"Thank you. If I have any issues, I'll let you know." With that, Bobbie stood, and she and Rafi left the room.

"What do you say to dinner out tonight?" Rafi asked Bobbie on Friday afternoon as Zain rode around the ring on Ransom.

"Dinner out?" Bobbie watched Zain. He had good carriage on the horse and was smiling.

"Yes." Rafi moved behind her, his arms coming around to rest next to hers on the rail, his chest against her back. "Wafi's has an excellent menu."

Heat invaded her body, and Bobbie swallowed. The week had flown, and while they'd spent most of their nights together, her body couldn't get enough of him. "Sounds like fun."

"Good." His breath ruffled her hair.

She'd enjoy a night out with him, even though she shouldn't. She pushed the negative thoughts away. Bobbie wanted to enjoy her time with Rafi even if nothing could come of it. For the first time in her life she felt truly free. "Is there a dress code?"

"No. Just dress for comfort. We'll leave at seven."

Bobbie nodded.

Rafi stood at the bottom of the stairs waiting for Bobbie when a sound had him glancing up. His mouth went dry, and his cock came to attention. Bobbie was absolutely beautiful. Her hair was up, and she wore a long floral print skirt with a white blouse.

"You take my breath away," Rafi said, taking her hand as she reached the bottom of the stairs.

She flushed with pleasure. "You're not bad yourself."

He grinned. The black pants and blue shirt had been a last-minute decision. Apparently a good one, going by the desire in her eyes.

"Thank you, my lady." He gave her a slight bow. "Our chariot awaits." Rafi slipped his arm around her waist and led her outside to where Hamaz, Ryan, and Barak stood. Barak was one of the newer security guards, but Rafi was glad to have him on the job. He wanted to make sure Bobbie was safe.

Within ten minutes, they exited the vehicle and walked into Wafi's. "Your Royal Highness, it is a pleasure to have you here tonight," the hostess said.

"Thank you," Rafi said.

"If you and your lady would follow me." The woman stood and held back the curtains around the entrance to the dining room. Rafi kept his hold around Bobbie's waist as he guided her into the room. Her gasp of delight made him smile.

"Oh, my, this is so ... I don't know what to call it."

"Authentic," he suggested. "I enjoy the warm bright colors and delicious aromas." He loved the feel of Wafi's. The way the light fixtures on the walls looked like old-fashioned oil lamps, the low tables in front of the stage, and the colorful throw pillows on the floor in front of the stage.

They were led to one of the high-backed booths. The

hostess gestured to the booth. "Here is your table. Please, enjoy your dinner."

"Thank you," Rafi said, as Bobbie slid into the booth. He followed, sliding into the booth until their thighs touched. The pressure of her body next to his aroused his senses.

She gestured toward the glass chandelier. "It's very beautiful."

"It is." He brought her hand to his lips and kissed the back of it. "Wafi's is known for the best food and entertainment."

A small shudder shook her body as he held her hand. "What kind of entertainment?" she asked.

"Musicians, and maybe some dancing." The image of Bobbie in his arms as they swayed made his dick jump.

"Sounds interesting." She tugged at her hand, but he held fast.

Wafi stepped up to their table and smiled. "Prince Rafi and Lady Roberta, I am pleased to have you grace my establishment tonight." He gave a little bow and then snapped his fingers. Water glasses were set on the table, along with little bowls of water and small hand towels. "Would you like wine tonight?"

"Yes, please. I think a bottle of your house red would be perfect," Rafi said as he released Bobbie's hand.

"Very good choice, Your Highness. Please refresh yourselves, and if you need anything at all, let me know." Wafi turned and bustled away.

Rafi turned to Bobbie, who was already washing her fingers in the bowl. He stared at her.

"What?" She dried off her fingers.

"You knew what to do?" He remembered Hassan mentioning how he had guided Sara through their dinner.

"I did study up a little bit on Bashir before I came so I would know some things."

Rafi cleaned his fingers. "And what else did you learn?" He was curious about her research.

"Let's see, you allow alcohol, there is very little crime, and the country has its traditions like this one." She gestured to the bowls.

Rafi let out a little laugh. "I assumed you researched the family." She was a teacher; of course she'd research the customs of the country she was coming to.

"Actually, no, I mainly just talked with Catherine about the job and a little bit about the family." She tilted her head. He reached up and caressed her neck, enjoying the feel of her soft skin beneath his fingertips.

A waiter approached. He set a platter of cheese, fruit, and nuts in front of them. "Wafi will be here shortly with your wine."

"Were you more interested in the job than the family?"

She gave a laugh. "Well, it is my job. I honestly didn't expect to be so involved with the family."

Rafi thought about her words as he looked over the food. She had a point. "There is a reason I chose Wafi's."

With his right hand he picked up a piece of melon and held it to her lips.

Bobbie's startled gaze met his. He'd caught her off guard by offering her food. Still he waited, holding it to her lips, until she opened her mouth and bit down on the watermelon. Rafi kept his gaze on her face, watching as she ate the ripe melon.

He waited until she swallowed the last of the sweet juice from her morsel and popped the rest of the slice of fruit in his mouth. His body heated at the intimate gesture of sharing food.

After he finished eating, she said, "Why did you do that?"

"I wanted to feed you from my hand. To take care of you, at least for one night." He wasn't sure where the words came from, but they were true.

"You do take care of me." Her hazel eyes softened, and she placed her hand on his face. "Every time we play or when we're in bed together your focus is on me."

"As it should be. Women are meant to be cherished."

The clearing of a male voice caused them both to jump. "Apologies, sir," the waiter said.

"It's all right," Rafi told him.

"Wafi sends with his compliments." The waiter set down two big bowls with large spoons and then two smaller bowls. "Wafi will be here with your wine shortly."

As he walked away, Wafi strode to the table with a bottle of wine and two glasses. He showed the bottle to

Rafi, who nodded; then Wafi poured the two glasses and left.

"The food smells amazing," Bobbie said.

"Let's see what we have." He touched the bowl closest to her. "Mejadra, lentils and rice with lots of spices, topped with crispy fried onions. And this," he touched the second bowl, "is one of Wafi's special dishes; the best translation is lamb stew."

Rafi dished it into one of the bowls. He took his spoon and dipped it in the lamb stew before holding it out to Bobbie. She opened her mouth and closed her lips around the utensil.

Her eyes went wide as she chewed and then swallowed. "Oh, my goodness, I can taste the cinnamon, paprika, and cayenne pepper. That is so good."

He smiled. "Then let us eat." Rafi would feed her a bite and then take one for himself. He loved the way she enjoyed her food, not like other women he'd been out with who would only take a bit here and there. They consumed all of the delicious food.

"Stop," she said when he held up another fork full of mejadra. "I can't. I'm so full."

Rafi nodded and ate the food on the fork, then pushed everything aside. "I'm sure Wafi will have dessert for us. Do you want some coffee to go with it?"

"That would be wonderful."

While they had some wine, there was still some left in

the bottle. The band came out and began playing. Rafi slipped his arm around Bobbie's shoulders.

She sat back and listened to the music, slightly swaying to the beat. Rafi loved the sounds of the flute and of the lute. Another man joined the band with a zorna, a double reed instrument, and then another with an oboe.

He let the music sweep over him. The low tones and sensual beat helped him relax and forget about everything but the music and the woman next to him.

"The music is beautiful," she said. "I need to find some to play in the classroom. I want Zain to have an appreciation of his country's music."

"Maybe I'll put some on during our next play session," he whispered. She tilted her head, and the desire in her eyes hit him in the groin.

"Are we going to play tonight?"

"I'd like to, if you're up for it."

"Oh." She moved her hand to his thigh and then closer to his cock. "I think you might be." She squeezed his dick, and he almost jumped out of the booth at how good having her hand on him was. He brushed his lips against hers as he tweaked her nipple.

"Excuse me." Rafi looked up to see Wafi standing by the table. "Dessert and coffee." The dinner dishes were cleared away and a platter was set on the table, along with a silver coffeepot, two cups, a creamer, and sugar. "Please enjoy, and you won't be disturbed again." Wafi smiled, then backed away.

Rafi glanced at Bobbie, and her cheeks were red. "Wafi didn't see anything except maybe my kiss," he said softly.

"I know, but … " Her hand patted his thigh.

"Sweetheart." He grinned before giving her another soft kiss. "There's nothing to be embarrassed about." He poured them both coffee, and added cream and sugar to hers, before looking at dessert. "Mshabak."

"It looks delicious. What is it?"

"Mshabak is a Lebanese sweet. Basically fried dough soaked in a sweet syrup."

"Some look like donuts and others are more like snail pastries."

"Yes, the dough is molded into circular shapes." He picked one up and held it to her mouth. Bobbie took a bite and moaned. The sound she made went straight to his dick.

After she swallowed, she said, "Delicious, covered in honey."

Rafi popped the rest of the dessert into his mouth. Bobbie's hand caught his, and she pulled his hand to her mouth. She pulled his fingers between her lips and sucked. Heat flooded his body. The woman was sensual beyond belief. From the way she enjoyed food to the way she enjoyed *him* …

When she released his fingers with a pop it was all he could do to stay in his seat. With an impatient wave he motioned the waiter over. "Could you wrap up the mshabak to go, please?"

"Of course, sir. Will only take a moment." The platter was whisked away.

Desire beat through his bloodstream much like the music playing. "Drink your coffee. As soon as the waiter is back we're leaving."

"As you wish, Sir." Her voice was low, but the 'sir' sent a shock wave through his body. While he wasn't hard into BDSM, just hearing that word from her lips did things to him.

Thank goodness the waiter was back within five minutes. Wafi would send the bill to the palace to be paid, so Rafi slid out of the booth and held out his hand for Bobbie. He tucked her close to his side as he picked up the box and led her to the exit. Wafi stood by the red-curtained exit.

"I hope all was to your satisfaction, Prince Rafi," he said, with a bow.

"It was wonderful as always," he said.

"Delicious dinner, Wafi. Thank you for the experience," Bobbie said.

Wafi smiled, took Bobbie's hand, and kissed the back of it. "I hope you and the prince will visit us again."

"Me too," Bobbie said.

Rafi nodded, then guided Bobbie out the entrance. They'd barely cleared the building when flashes went off in their faces. Bobbie gave a small cry at the paparazzi.

Hamaz pushed his way to them along with Barak. "Sorry, Prince Rafi," Hamaz said as he reached the couple.

"Where the hell did they come from?" Barak asked. "They weren't here a few minutes ago."

"Who knows," Rafi said, shoving the box of food into Barak's hands. "Let's just get to the car."

"Prince Rafi, are you dating Miss Anderson?" a reporter yelled.

"Miss Anderson, how does it feel dating the prince?" another one yelled.

"The pictures of the two of you at the wedding are stunning. So are you two an item?" another yelled.

"What pictures?" Bobbie asked quietly.

Rafi shook his head and kept her close. Ryan stood at the SUV with the door open. They slid inside, and the door was shut. Rafi was behind the driver, Bobbie in the middle and Ryan next to her. Samir and Barak climbed in the front next to the driver, and they were off.

"What did they mean about the wedding photos?" Bobbie repeated.

Rafi glanced at her. Confusion was written on her face. He let out a breath. "This wasn't how I planned tonight."

Her soft hand touched his. "Tell me, Rafi."

"When I escorted you from the SUV up the stairs the photographers took pictures."

"Okay, so why are the press making such a big deal out of it?"

Ryan let out a laugh, and Bobbie turned her head to him. "Ryan?"

"Sorry, Prince Rafi will explain."

"It was more of us coming out. Remember when we paused on the stairs?" he asked.

"Yes, we stopped for a moment as Catherine and Malik exited the church." Her nose scrunched up.

"We did. We turned, and I kept you close to my side as we looked back at them."

"We did, and ... oh, hell's bells."

Rafi grinned. "The photographers caught the moment when you glanced up at me, and I looked down at you." He'd forgotten the moment until Khalid had showed him the paper on Monday.

The photographer had caught them at the perfect moment, staring into each other's eyes, like a couple so madly in love they only had eyes for each other. Rafi had chosen not to show Bobbie the paper. The press was only speculating. He hadn't expected them tonight, although he should have. Didn't what had happened with Hassan and Sara teach him anything?

"So they took a picture. I'm guessing it was in the paper," she said, her voice low.

"It was."

"I see." She crossed her arms over her chest. "And you chose not to tell me."

"I did." He wasn't going to lie to her. "I wanted to protect you."

Bobbie took a deep breath and then looked at him. "You can protect me by letting me know what is happening. I wouldn't have been so surprised by the photographers tonight."

Rafi nodded. "True."

"So now what do we do?" she asked.

"What do you mean?"

"Somehow I have a feeling the pictures they took and some article are going to appear in tomorrow's paper. My question is, do we do anything about it?"

"You are not mad?" In her situation, he would be hot under the collar.

"Disappointed you didn't tell me, but not mad. How could you know those idiots would show up?"

"You are wonderful." Rafi leaned down and gave her a quick kiss.

"Oh, you're not out of the woods yet, but I really feel we need a plan of action."

His heart squeezed. He loved how she stood up to him. And it made the next words even more pleasing to utter. "We do. How do you feel about becoming engaged?"

"Absolutely not," Bobbie said, pacing around Malik's office. They'd returned from dinner to find Malik and Khalid waiting for them.

"Why not?" Rafi asked, his gaze following her every move.

"Because it's just not possible." She waved her hands in the air. "I'm Zain's teacher. I'm not royal material." Even as she protested, a part of her wanted to agree to being engaged to Rafi. Damn, she was getting in too deep. Maybe the press had done her a favor.

"But," Rafi started.

"No, Rafi," Malik said in a firm voice. "Bobbie has spoken. We will figure this out."

Rafi crossed his arms over his chest, clearly not happy. Well, that was his problem. She couldn't become engaged to him, fake or not. She was broken. Bobbie hugged herself as familiar pain invaded her bones.

"Why not just tell them we're dating and leave it at that?" she asked.

"That was our next option," Khalid said.

"Then why not use it?" She fought against fears. It was impossible to give in to the idea of their being engaged.

"It doesn't give you the same protection as an engagement does." Malik held up his hand when she opened her mouth to speak again. "But since you spend your time here at the palace or on the palace grounds, I think we're good."

Bobbie nodded and then glanced at Rafi. His features were closed down. She rubbed her hands over her chilled arms. "If you'll excuse me, I'm going to bed." She left the room.

Once inside her bedroom, Bobbie kicked off her shoes and stripped off her clothes. The night had started out so promising. Now it was a mess. Tears gathered in her eyes.

No doubt her relationship with Rafi had changed tonight. She sighed and pushed her negative thoughts away. It was what it was. Life wasn't always how we wanted it, and she would cope as she'd done all her life.

She slipped into the bathroom. When she emerged and moved back into her bedroom a shaft of disappointment shot through her. She'd expected Rafi to be there waiting for her.

Well, they apparently weren't going to play or anything

else tonight. Crossing the room, she opened the drawer, pulled out a nightshirt, and slipped it on. Maybe tomorrow he would be in a better mood.

Rafi fumed as Khalid and Malik discussed how they could spin this to the press. What was wrong with Bobbie? Okay, maybe a fake engagement wasn't the best thing, but damn it, he was in love with her.

He went still. He was in love with Bobbie? Yes, he was. Why hadn't he realized it until now? It had grown gradually, but every day he found himself looking forward to being with her, to seeing her.

"Sounds like a plan. Rafi?" Malik's voice penetrated his distraction.

"What? Sorry."

Khalid laughed and Malik grinned. "We were just saying, we'll let the press run with their story and let it go at that. You two were only out to dinner, and the wedding pictures are just that, wedding pictures."

Rafi nodded. "And if the press starts digging?"

"I saw nothing in her background that would cause an issue," Khalid said.

But she was hiding something. Rafi felt it in his bones. Bobbie had a secret. One she didn't want to share with him. "Fine," he said as he stood. "We'll probably have the paparazzi camped out around the palace for a while."

"Yes," Khalid said. "I'll increase the guards."

"Catherine is not going to be happy. We have several events next week." Malik rubbed his forehead.

"Tell her I'm sorry." Catherine was getting better with the press, but Rafi knew if she never had to deal with them again, she'd be happy.

"Not your fault," Malik said. "I'll be with her, and she's better when I'm with her."

Rafi nodded. "Someone needs to inform Hassan and Sara. They're visiting one of the village clinics next week," he said.

"I will," Khalid said. "Hassan and I were meeting in the morning to discuss security, so we can discuss it then."

"Very well." Rafi left Malik's office and went to his room. Part of him wanted to go to Bobbie's room, but he decided not to. He'd give her some time.

The next afternoon, Rafi was in the stables mucking out the stalls. He needed to do something. Bobbie had refused to talk with him. She'd taken breakfast in her room; then, when he knocked on her door, she didn't answer.

The classroom door was closed, and when he looked in, she wasn't there. No one seemed to know where she was, and he was beyond frustrated. How could she disappear on the palace grounds?

He'd questioned the guards at the gate, and they'd assured him she hadn't left. He'd even checked with Hamaz, and he hadn't seen her. Malik, Catherine, and

Zain had gone into Bashir City to the marketplace. Hassan and Sara were at the hospital.

Rafi decided to work off his frustration by mucking out the stalls. Usually Razan or another stable hand did it, but he needed to do something before he started tearing the palace apart to find Bobbie.

Why was she hiding from him? The question bounced around in his mind. Was she that upset he'd suggested an engagement? If so, why? Over the last few months they'd gotten to know each other pretty well.

He shook his head. There was no figuring out women. His mind turned to when he was in college and with his longtime girlfriend. Rafi cut his thoughts off. No, he wasn't going to go back there. It was his past; this was his future.

After laying new hay and straw he shut the stall door and headed for the tack room. There was a note tacked on the door. That was odd. He took it off and opened it. The opening line was from one of the stable hands; it read: *My second cousin asked me to leave this for you. He said it was important.* Rafi read the rest of the note. It was his informant. He wanted to meet that night. He'd given Rafi the location.

Well, at least that would be something to do besides moping around waiting to see Bobbie. Rafi put everything away and made his way toward the palace. He'd shower and then take out Shadow.

Rafi hid behind the outcropping of rocks and watched the men around the fire. His contact hadn't shown up, but these men had. So Rafi stayed hidden and tried to hear their conversation, but he was only getting bits and pieces.

After two hours the men put out the fire, packed up, and left. The snippets Rafi had heard in their conversation were enough. He was worried about his contact, but it was possible he hadn't been able to get away.

He stood and stretched out his cramped muscles before making his way back to where he had left Shadow. The time out in the desert had given him time to think and clear his head.

Why Bobbie wouldn't agree to a fake engagement was no longer an issue. Now that he'd calmed down a bit, he could understand why she wouldn't want to be in the spotlight all the time. Not that them being an item wouldn't create a stir.

Rafi mounted Shadow and off they went back toward Bashir City and the palace. He'd find Bobbie tomorrow, and he would tell her he understood. He'd missed her today, and he wanted to be with her no matter what.

Once back, he brushed Shadow down and crept into the palace. Inside his room, he changed his clothes and wrote out a note for Khalid. Before going downstairs to put it in Khalid's office, Rafi snuck into Bobbie's room.

He couldn't wait until morning to see her. Rafi stood in her bedroom door watching her sleep. Her dark hair was spread out over her pillow, and one leg was out from under the covers as she slept.

Rafi felt a sense of peace invade his body. Yes, he'd missed her. Yes, he was in love with her. And yes, he'd find a way to make things work. Because one thing had become very clear tonight. He didn't want to lose her. He turned and left her room.

Once downstairs, he made his way to Khalid's office. He'd already made note of the camera Khalid had installed. He'd drop off the notes, get a few hours' rest, and then start *Operation Bobbie*. Rafi set the note on Khalid's desk and turned.

"Rafi?" Khalid's voice held surprise.

Rafi raised his gaze to the ceiling. "Khalid, what are you doing up?" Oh, hell, how was he going to bluff his way out of this?

"Waiting for my mysterious note person. I didn't expect it to be you."

"What makes you think it's me?"

Khalid laughed, turned on the small lamp by his desk, and removed the night vision goggles from his face. When had his brother moved? Damn, the man was good.

"Besides the fact I've been in this room the whole time?" Khalid picked up the note and read it quickly. "Want to tell me why the notes? And how you've been getting this information?"

"And if I say no?" Rafi stared at his brother.

"Then I guess I'll just tickle it out of you like I did when we were kids."

Instinctively Rafi took a step back and covered his sides. "Damn it, Khalid, we're not children anymore."

"Well, it's either that, or I throw my brother in jail for spying, so what's it going to be?"

"I had to do something," Rafi said in his defense.

Khalid gestured to the chair, and Rafi sat down as Khalid took his place behind his desk. "You're the second-born son, too valuable."

"I'm just the spare." Rafi gave a laugh. He'd always called himself the spare since he was little, not that he minded. Malik was suited to be king.

"You're more than that. Mom would have your hide if she knew what you were doing."

"Which is why no one can find out." Rafi took a deep breath. "After Sara's near kidnapping, I decided to see if I could find out more about Kalif's operation."

"On your own?" Khalid asked, with raised eyebrows.

"Yes. Everyone is used to my being at the stables at different times." And it was true, he enjoyed being with his horses and making sure they were well. "So it was simple enough to slip out at night on Shadow and see what I could find out."

Khalid nodded. "Why leave me notes? Why not come to me with the information?"

Rafi laughed. "Really, brother? If I had, what would have you done?"

Khalid closed his eyes and then opened them. "Stopped you."

"Right. I made friends with one of the men in the village closest to Kalif's new operation. He's been slipping me information when he can. Last night I was supposed to meet him, but Kalif's men showed up."

"A trap?" Khalid sat up straighter.

"I don't think so, they just sat around the fire talking. They didn't even search for anyone. I was too far away to catch the entire conversation, but got bits and pieces. After a few hours, they left. So if they were planning a trap, it was poorly executed."

"Well, I for one am happy for that. No more, Rafi."

"I can't promise that, Khalid." Rafi held up his hands. "I'm careful."

Khalid let out a sigh. "I can't stop you—well, I could, but it would create an uproar in the household."

"Thank you."

"The next time you go out, tell me or Hamaz. At least this way if you don't come back, we know to go look for you." Khalid stood, strode over to him, and clapped him on the shoulder. "Mom would have a fit if anything happened to you."

"And you too." Rafi returned the embrace.

The brothers parted ways, and Rafi climbed the stairs to his room. But he didn't want to be alone. He went back to Bobbie's room, stripped down to his underwear, and climbed into bed next to her.

He'd done this before when he'd been working late or after a quick meeting with his informant. Rafi turned to gather her into his arms and saw Bobbie staring at him.

"Do you want me to leave?"

"No." She lifted her hand and cupped his cheek. "I'm sorry I overreacted to the fake engagement."

"I think I understand why you did," he said softly as he pulled her into his embrace. "Go back to sleep."

"You're a wonderful man, Rafi. Any woman would be happy to be your wife." Her lashes drifted shut and her breathing evened out.

"Except the woman in my arms," he whispered.

Three days later, Bobbie smiled at Zain. He'd finished his work, and he was bouncing in his seat. She was aware of what he wanted to do.

"All right, Zain," she said, stacking the papers on her desk. She could grade them later. "Let's go down to the stables."

Zain jumped up and ran to the door, then stopped and waited for her. Bobbie took his hand. Together they found Hamaz and walked down to the stables. Almost every afternoon, Bobbie took Zain to the stables.

Zain loved being around the horses, and it gave her a chance to see Rafi. At the stables, they found Rafi in the training ring. They watched him with the horses for a little bit before he noticed them and walked over to them.

"My favorite lady." He swept a kiss over her lips. "And my favorite little man." He picked Zain up and spun him around. Zain's laughter filled Bobbie with joy. He'd had a hard life until fate brought him Catherine and Malik. Rafi set Zain down and said, "I take it you would like to ride Ransom?"

Zain nodded his head.

"Okay, you know what to go do. Make sure Razan helps you with the saddle."

Zain ran off and Bobbie laughed. "All that energy," she said, as she turned to Rafi. "Where did you go last night?"

"I had to be up early this morning and didn't want to disturb you."

"You disturb me all the time," she said, then grinned. Since they'd talked on Sunday things were better between them.

"Oh, then—" A high-pitched screech filled the air. "Fire!" The word had barely left his mouth and they were both running for the stables.

Razan was sitting outside the stables when they rounded the corner. "Razan, where is Zain?" Rafi asked as he knelt down next to the man.

"I didn't see him." Razan coughed.

"Zain." Bobbie didn't hesitate; she ran into the barn as Hamaz yelled her name. There was lots of smoke, but she couldn't see or smell a fire. The horses were pawing at the stable doors. Ransom's stall was about halfway down.

Spying a rag hanging on the first stall, she grabbed it and tied it over her mouth and nose. She opened the stall doors as she went. When she reached Ransom's stall, her heart almost stopped. The horse's eyes were wide with fear, his ears were laid back, and Zain was in the corner.

Bobbie forced herself to stay calm. She couldn't see but a few feet in front of her, but there was no orange glow of a fire. Carefully, she opened the stall door. Zain lifted his head, but he didn't move. Good. She stepped inside. The smoke wasn't heavy in Ransom's stall, so that was a good thing.

"Don't move, Zain, everything will be okay," she said quietly. "It's okay, Ransom." She kept her voice soft and her tone gentle. "It's just the fire alarm, nothing is going to hurt you." As she talked she edged her way into the stall, keeping her back to the wall and her eyes on Ransom.

"Easy boy." She found the rope they used to lead the horses out of the stall and lifted it off the wall. It was heavier than she remembered. "It's okay, Ransom, I'll get you and Zain out of here."

The smoke was clearing a little, but that didn't mean there wasn't a fire somewhere. "I won't hurt you, Ransom." She kept talking to him as she approached. Thank goodness she'd been with Zain when he rode the horse. The horse was familiar with her.

Ransom's ears were more alert now and facing front.

He was still agitated, but calmer. "Good boy." Bobbie uncoiled the rope and slipped the loop over the horse's head. Ransom stayed still as if understanding she was trying to help him.

Once she had the rope on, she backed up until she reached Zain's side. "Zain, honey, can you get up?" The boy shook his head. "Are you hurt?" Damn, how could she get them both out?

Zain shook his head no. She took a breath and knelt down. Zain threw himself into her arms, almost knocking her over. "It's okay, baby." Zain was shaking like a leaf. And that's when she remembered he'd been in a fire before. "Oh, damn," she swore.

Bobbie looked at the stall door. There was more smoke than ever. She could hear people shouting and voices, but she wasn't sure where they were. With a deep breath, Bobbie stood, adjusting Zain against her.

The boy was solid, but she could carry him. Carefully she made her way to the stall door. She poked her head out. Only smoke, no orange glow that she could see, and the smoke was white. Thick but white. Zain started coughing.

Time for them to get out of there. "Come on, Ransom," she said, pulling the lead as she stepped outside the stall. The smoke burned her eyes and made her nose twitch even with the cloth over it. "Keep your eyes closed, Zain. Bury your face against my shirt and breathe through your nose."

That would help him a little bit with the smoke, but not her. She kept close to the stall doors, using them as a guide. Her eyes began to water, making it hard to see, and she was fighting not to cough. Suddenly there was someone in front of her.

"My lady." Hamaz took her by the arm after taking Ransom's lead from her hand and led them out the entrance of the barn.

Bobbie stepped outside, and the fresh air cascaded over her face, causing her to start coughing. Zain wiggled in her hold. She set him down and pulled the makeshift mask off her face as she bent over trying to catch her breath.

"Easy, Bobbie," Hassan said, trying to place an oxygen mask over her face.

Bobbie pushed his hand away. "Check Zain, we've got to get the rest of the horses out."

"It's being done. You need oxygen." He slapped the mask over her mouth and nose and held it there.

She took a few deep breaths, then said, "Where's Rafi?"

"Right here." His arms encircled her from behind. His hold was firm.

"Zain?" She looked at the little boy who was sitting on the ground with Sara. "I need to make sure he's okay."

Hassan looked over her shoulder. Bobbie pushed the oxygen mask away and twisted her head to talk to Rafi.

The stark fear in his eyes almost made her knees buckle. "Please Rafi, let me check on Zain."

He nodded, but instead of releasing her as she expected, he picked her up in his arms and carried her over to Zain. Once he put her on her feet, Bobbie sank down next to Zain. "Are you okay, my little man?" She ruffled his hair, her heart pounding.

Zain was in her lap in a shot, hugging her close. "I was so scared, but you saved me," he whispered.

Bobbie's mouth dropped open, but she shut it quickly. Zain had spoken to her. She calmed her racing heart and swallowed. If she made too big of deal out of it, he might not talk more. She took a deep breath before speaking. "I was scared too." She held the shaking boy close to her. Her gaze met Rafi's. His eyes still held fear, but there was something else there, and she couldn't put a name to it.

Fighting the urge to gather Bobbie back into his arms, Rafi stood staring at her, his entire body shaking with fear. When she'd run into the stable before he could stop her, his heart had almost stopped beating. He'd grabbed one of the wet rags Hamaz had held out to him and dived in after her.

The smoke had been thick and the horses were shrieking along with the smoke alarms. He couldn't see Bobbie in the barn. He'd find her and then deal with the horses. No signs of flames, only smoke. He tried making his way to Ransom's stall. But one of the stall doors was kicked open as he passed.

The door caught him in the hip and spun him around. Orion, the horse, panicked and ran straight at Rafi. He jumped to the side, but was clipped by the horse. He started to go down as Hamaz grabbed him and pulled him out of the stable. After Hamaz had dumped him outside, the bodyguard ran back in.

Rafi was just getting to his feet to run back in when Hassan, Sara, Khalid, and the security force arrived. Khalid refused to let him back into the barn. Instead they went to the opposite side and opened the doors. When he returned, Bobbie was out.

"There was no fire," Khalid said, coming up to his side.

"But the smoke," Rafi said.

"Smoke bombs." Khalid held up a small canister.

"But why?" Rafi shook his head. "All they would do is set off the alarms."

"Yes, and bring everyone running."

"Because the alarms would frighten the horses."

Khalid nodded. It dawned on Rafi this could be a diversion.

"Where are Catherine and Malik?" Damn it, was this another attempt on Catherine?

"Safe. I left four guards with them in Malik's office. He wasn't happy. Plus I made sure Mom and Dad were in there too."

"Thank you, brother. I bet Malik is chomping at the bit." Rafi's gaze went back to Bobbie and Zain.

"Zain spoke."

"What?" Khalid shook his head. "Did you just say Zain spoke?"

"Yes. When Bobbie sat down next to him, he jumped into her arms and told her he was scared." Rafi shook his head. Bobbie had accomplished something they'd been working on for months.

Zain would whisper to Catherine or Malik but nothing anyone else could hear. This time Rafi had heard the words even as softly as they were spoken. Razan, one of the stable hands, walked up to them.

"I don't know what happened, sir," Razan said, giving a little bow.

"What do you remember?" Khalid asked.

"Zain came in and went to Ransom's stall. I knew he wanted to ride. I went into the tack room to grab his saddle and then nothing."

"Someone was hiding in the tack room?" Rafi glanced around to see if he could see anyone out of place. No, the other stable hands were there, calming the horses and leading them to the pasture.

"I believe so." Razan rubbed the back of his head. "I don't think I was out long. When I woke there was smoke and the alarm was going off. Then I stepped outside the tack room and I was overwhelmed." He looked up at Rafi. "Forgive me, sir. I didn't realize little Zain was inside, otherwise I never would have stumbled outside."

"It's okay, Razan." Rafi touched the young man's shoulder. "Have Hassan check you out."

"Is our home no longer safe?" Rafi asked his brother as Razan walked away.

The radio at Khalid's waist went off. He pulled it out, listened and spoke. "The guards have checked everywhere, but no one came in or out that doesn't belong. This doesn't make sense—it has to be someone working for us. I'll figure it out." Khalid rubbed the back of his neck. "Why don't you take Bobbie and Zain up to the palace? I'm sure Catherine and Malik are going crazy."

Rafi nodded and took a step before Khalid's voice stopped him. "And remind Bobbie that running into a burning stable is crazy."

"Oh, we will be talking about it." Rafi strode over to Bobbie.

"What possessed you to run into the stable?" Rafi asked two hours later. Maybe asked wasn't the right word. More like demanded.

"It was instinct." Bobbie ran a brush through her hair. After talking about Zain to Malik and Catherine, Bobbie had retreated to her room to clean up.

"Instinct?" Rafi pulled the brush from her grasp and began brushing her hair. He might have been angry with her, but his strokes were gentle.

"I can't explain it, Rafi. I knew Zain was in there, and I had to get him out. Let alone the horses. They are valuable."

"Not as valuable as you."

Their gazes met in the mirror where she sat at the vanity table. "Rafi." Bobbie lifted her hand and touched his where it rested on her shoulder. "I've dealt with a stable fire before."

A shiver went through her body. It hadn't ended as well as this one, but it had been a long time ago. And she wasn't being silly when she told Rafi it was instinct. She'd acted on autopilot from her father's teachings. People first, then the horses, both at the same time if you can.

"When?" he asked softly, as he finished brushing her hair.

"I was about twelve. Remember, my father raised horses. There was a bad storm and we thought lightening hit the stable. I helped him get the horses out." She swallowed, remembering the smoke and the red-orange glow of the flames. "We got all but two out. It wasn't until after the fire department arrived that we found one of the stable hands. He apparently had been smoking and fell asleep. The hay caught fire."

The brush was set on the vanity, and Rafi pulled her to her feet and enveloped her into his arms. "I had to get to Zain. Malik and Catherine would never have forgiven me if something happened to that sweet boy."

Tears filled her eyes and slid down her cheeks when she thought about how dangerous today's events had been.

"And I could never have forgiven myself," she whispered.

"Baby." Rafi walked them backward until he sat on the bed with her in his lap.

"I didn't mean to scare you. I knew Zain would be in Ransom's stall. There was so much smoke, but I didn't smell fire or see it."

"I understand." He rubbed her back in a soothing motion.

"I'd forgotten about Zain being in a fire before until I saw his face. He was so scared. Ransom was too. So I calmed Ransom down, got the lead over his neck, and then picked up Zain."

"He's heavy."

"Yeah, he is." Bobbie wiped her tears away with the sleeve of her robe. "I couldn't leave either of them. Thankfully, Hamaz found us, took Ransom, and led us out."

"Yes." A shudder ran through Rafi's body, and Bobbie looked up at him.

"Are you okay?"

"I am, but I want you to promise me you'll never do something like that again." He pulled her closer to him. "My heart almost stopped beating when you ran into the stable."

"I'm sorry." She was. She'd never meant to scare him. She hadn't been kidding when she told him she was acting on instinct. Her only thought had been to get Zain out of there.

Rafi's lips caressed her temple. "I want to spank you for being so brave," he whispered.

Hot tendrils of need wound their way through her veins. "What is stopping you?" Where had those words come from?

He put some space between them and looked at her. "What did you say?" His eyes narrowed, but not before she saw passion flare in them.

"I think you heard me." She slipped off his lap and stood in front of him. "If you wish to punish me, then do so."

"Not punishment." His words were soft. "Pleasure, only pleasure." He stood and stripped off her robe.

Bobbie shifted on the hard chair at breakfast the next morning. Her ass was still tender from Rafi's punishment from last night. If you could call it that. Heat filled her. He did spank her, quite nicely, then he brought her to climax with his fingers before tucking her against him and telling her to sleep.

Each time she'd woken last night from a nightmare of not being able to reach Zain, Rafi was there, holding her close and reminding her Zain was fine. Her heart squeezed; it was amazing to be cared for by him.

She was just finishing up when Malik strode in.

"Good morning, Bobbie. I hope no after-effects from yesterday?" He poured himself a cup of coffee from the urn on the buffet.

Bobbie's eyes widened. What did Malik know about her and Rafi and their play last night? When he turned around he stared at her. "What you did yesterday in saving Zain was brave and foolish."

She blew out a breath of relief when she realized what he was talking about. "I know," she said. "I just reacted."

"I know both Catherine and I told you yesterday how grateful we are." He held up his hand when she opened her mouth. "I mean it, Bobbie. Zain is special to us. To the family. You risked your life to save his."

"But there was no fire."

"You had no way of knowing that when you rushed into the barn. I'm sure both Rafi and Khalid impressed upon you their displeasure at your doing something so foolish."

She nodded, although Rafi's displeasure had been more pleasurable than Khalid's talk yesterday. Khalid wanted her to understand they had measures in place, and she was not to put herself in danger again. His voice had been hard, but there had also been a hint of respect in his eyes.

"Good. Now, Zain is resting. He had a bad night."

"Nightmares?" The poor little guy.

"Yes. Catherine is with him, but he's been asking for you. Would you mind going and sitting with him for a while?"

"Of course not. I'm sure Catherine has a million and one things to do." Bobbie finished her coffee and stood. When she went to pass Malik, he put his hand on her arm.

"Your sacrifice will not be forgotten." Malik gave her a quick hug, then released her before he turned and left the room.

Bobbie shook her head at Malik's words. Why did the family feel they owed her? She had done what anyone would have done. Bobbie made her way to the classroom. She'd grab a couple of books for her and Zain to read.

Rafi and Khalid went over every inch of the stable that morning, and they could find nothing to give them a clue about who had set off the smoke bombs. Khalid had his core security staff questioning everyone.

"Rafi," Khalid said.

"Yes." Rafi lifted his head from the stall where one of the smoke bombs had been. That was the other curious thing. The smoke bombs had been put in empty stalls.

"Are all of your stable hands accounted for?" Khalid asked.

"Yes, they're all here." Rafi thought about who was

here and who wasn't. "Wait—there are two that are off today, Musad and Umar."

"Their files are in my office," Khalid said. "Ryan, please go pull their addresses, and take Basam and two others with you. I want you to find both and bring them here."

"Yes, sir."

"You don't think?" Rafi shook his head.

"I don't want to, but someone had to put these in here, and they are the only two not here today. I've talked to everyone else. They were busy with their duties. The only one in the stables was Razan."

"All the staff has been vetted," Rafi said.

"Yes, but that doesn't mean they can't be bought."

"But it doesn't make sense, Khalid." Rafi rubbed the back of his neck. "There was no fire, no one was hurt."

"That's what is curious. I thought it might have been a distraction, but so far I haven't figured anything out."

"I believe I might have the answer to that," Razan said, walking up to the pair with something in his hand. "I found this tacked onto the stable door this morning."

He handed the paper to Khalid, who opened it and read it, then swore. "Why didn't you bring this to me earlier?"

Razan looked at the ground. "I'm sorry, sir. I had work to do and just thought it was from one of the other workers. I didn't read it until just now."

Rafi touched the worker's shoulder. "It's okay, Razan,

you had no way of knowing. Thank you for bringing this to us."

Razan nodded and left. Rafi turned to his brother. "Razan has been working at the stables since he was a boy. He is not a threat. What did the note say?"

"I know, sorry. I'm tense." He handed the note to Rafi.

Rafi read it. "*I have people everywhere. Back off or there will be more accidents. K.*"

"He's threatening us." Rafi almost couldn't believe Kalif's nerve, but then again, they were taking away his source of income.

"I will not stop. I will rid our country of this vermin," Khalid said in a tight voice.

"We will." Just then Hassan came striding over to the pair. "Now what?" Rafi asked.

"The press is going nuts. Malik wants to hold a press conference," Hassan said.

Khalid nodded. "Same protocols we've had in place. Everyone is to be searched and only one way into the room and one way out for the press."

This time Khalid's cell phone rang; he answered it and frowned. "Yes, thank you, Ryan. Take care of everything and keep it as quiet as you can."

"What did Ryan find?" Rafi asked.

"Umar is dead." Khalid ran a hand over his face. "He left a note saying he was suppose to set the barn on fire, and he's the one who left the note from Kalif. He is sorry but he had no choice."

"No choice? Everyone has a choice." Rafi shook his head. He'd trusted Umar; they all had.

"Apparently Kalif was using Umar's wife as collateral. They found her body in another part of their apartment. It looks like she's was killed a few hours before Umar."

"This is crazy; Kalif is using the people to do his dirty deeds," Hassan said.

"It won't last for long," Khalid said.

"No, I'll start spreading the word about what happened. We're getting more people to speak up. The people of Bashir will not put up with this," Rafi said. The people were proud, and they would rally to help. "In the meantime, how long until this press conference?"

"It's being arranged right now. Malik wants everyone there, and by everyone that includes Bobbie," Hassan said.

Rafi let out a sigh. "I'll go tell her the good news."

Five minutes later, Bobbie asked, "But why do I need to be there?"

"Malik wants everyone there." Rafi watched her pace. "Bobbie, why do you dislike the press?"

She turned to him. "I don't, I just don't like being in the limelight." She rubbed her hands up and down her arms like she was cold.

"I'll be there with you. The entire family except our parents will be there."

"Are your parents okay?"

"Yes, they left for the summer palace. It's actually safer for them there."

"Why? What is going on, Rafi?"

He'd debated telling her about the note, but then decided it would be a good thing. If someone tried to get to Zain or her, it would be better if she were aware. "Come, let's sit down." He cupped her elbow and led her over to the sofa. "Remember when I told you about the poppy growing," he said after they sat.

She wrinkled her nose. "I remember."

"Well, Kalif, who is in charge of the operation, is growing bolder in attacking us."

"Because you are trying to stop him."

"Yes. The smoke bombs were a warning."

"But with all your security." She waved her hands in the air.

"Yes, Khalid is beside himself. One of the stable hands was coerced into planting the smoke bombs."

"I don't like all this political intrigue."

"We don't, either." He shook his head. "But we've got Kalif confined to one area now. Once his forces are weakened, we'll go in and get him out."

"We?" she asked.

"Khalid and the security force." He wanted her to understand she was safe here, even if he was being overly cautious in warning her. "Khalid has been hiring more and more security and training them on the outskirts of Bashir City. Once they're fully trained, they're going to shut down Kalif. His days are numbered."

"Okay, but in the meantime, why do I need to be at this press conference?"

Rafi shook his head. "Solidarity. Plus it would show everyone that the family doesn't fear what is happening. We are stronger than ever."

"But I'm not family."

"In my eyes you are," Rafi said softly. "Bobbie, you mean a lot to me. You must know that."

She nodded. "You mean a lot to me too." Her voice was quiet.

"Good. You don't have to say a word or do anything but stand there. Okay?"

"I guess."

"Don't fear, my lovely sexy woman."

Bobbie took a deep breath as she walked into the press room with Rafi and the rest of the family. Her heart was beating so fast she was afraid she'd pass out. The buzz of voices became louder.

It's okay, she reminded herself. *This isn't like when you were sixteen and had to go through the inquiry into your father's death and his gambling.* This was different. This time she had support, not a mother who couldn't have cared less and friends who walked away.

Malik walked up to the podium, and the room quieted. "Thank you for being here. As you know, there was an incident at the stables yesterday. I'm happy to report it was a simple accident." Bobbie stiffened next to Rafi, and he squeezed her hand. "Someone set off some smoke bombs as a joke, and it created quite an issue."

Hands shot up in the air. This was much different than she remembered, heck, even from the other night; these reporters were not shouting out questions, but raising their hands. Malik pointed to one man.

"King Malik, with all these unusual accidents happening over the last six months, are you and the family at risk?"

"We're always at risk," Malik answered. "But it has been unusual, and I suspect they will slowly stop in the next few months." He pointed to another reporter.

"Prince Hassan, when are you and Lady Sara going to be wed?"

Sara laughed. "When we're ready. You just had one royal wedding, don't be in a hurry for another," she said.

Malik pointed to a female reporter. "Prince Rafi, are you and Lady Bobbie an item? And will there be a third royal engagement?"

Bobbie stiffened again, and Rafi squeezed her hand. "Bobbie and I are, I guess you could say, dating, as if a royal can date without the press hounding his every move."

The press laughed. More questions were shouted out but mainly about events coming up. Within ten minutes the press conference was wrapped up, and they left the room.

"Well, that was pleasant as ever," Catherine said, sinking down on to the sofa in the family area.

"It could have been worse," Sara said, dropping onto a chair.

"Really?" Bobbie couldn't imagine. "I hope I never have to go through it again." She really hated being in the public eye, and that was funny considering she was a teacher, but it felt different to her with students and their parents. They weren't really strangers to her as the press was.

Malik took a drink over to his wife and Hassan took one to Sara. Bobbie looked up at Rafi, and he held up a bottle of wine, but she shook her head. She wasn't much of a drinker, and right now she didn't want alcohol to muddle her thoughts. "Is it always like that?"

"Yes," Catherine answered.

"No," Sara answered at the same time.

"Don't let it get to you, Bobbie," Khalid said, as Rafi handed her a glass of mineral water. "Just ignore the press as best you can."

"Yes," Catherine said, "and you're lucky as you're mostly here in the palace. The rest of us are out where they're always yelling questions and taking pictures."

Bobbie nodded. Catherine was right, she was protected here. Not that she didn't believe the others weren't. If there was one thing she'd learned in the last few months, it was that the royal family protected their own and anyone they thought under their protection.

"Let's talk about a more pleasant thing," Sara said. "I understand Bashir City is going to have a celebration in a few months."

Khalid let out a groan. "Yes, the three-hundred-year anniversary of Bashir and the founding of Bashir City. It's going to be a security nightmare."

Malik shook his head. "All will be well, brother. We only have certain events we have to attend, and remember we won't announce which ones we will be at and which ones we won't. That will keep things a bit easier."

"Yes."

"A three-hundred-year anniversary?" Bobbie tilted her head. "I thought Bashir was founded well over a thousand years ago."

"It was," Malik said. "But at that time we were a part of other countries. We actually didn't become our own country until three hundred years ago."

Bobbie sat back, and Rafi put his arm around her shoulders as Malik talked about Bashir's history.

As she rested against Rafi, Bobbie placed her hand on her flat stomach. What would it be like to carry Rafi's child? She closed her eyes and took a breath. Why was she torturing herself with those kinds of thoughts? Natural-born children were not in her future.

"Miss Bobbie," Zain said. It had been a week since the stable incident. A week of the press trying to capture pictures of her and Rafi. Her nerves were running thin.

"Yes, Zain." The only good thing to come out of all of it was Zain was now talking.

"Are you and Rafi going to get married?"

"What?" Bobbie stared at Zain. "Why do you think that?" She toned her voice down.

Zain grinned at her. "I think it would be great if you did."

Bobbie didn't know what to say. Not that she hadn't entertained the idea of her and Rafi getting married. But it didn't seem to be in the cards.

"It would be fun to have a little brother or sister to play

with." Zain stacked his books in a neat pile. "I always wanted a baby brother, but my father refused."

Zain's words plunged a knife into her heart. The boy had suffered so much in his short life. His father had killed his mother, then set fire to their home to cover up the crime. What she wouldn't do to give Zain a friend to play with. But it wasn't meant to be. Zain would have to get friends to play with from Catherine and Sara.

He jumped up from his desk. "Can we go to the stables now?"

Bobbie shook her head. Like any seven-year-old, he would jump from one subject to the next. "All right." He was good for her. Caring for the children of others fulfilled her maternal needs, and Zain in particular nourished that part of her.

"You've been very quiet tonight," Bobbie said to Rafi after dinner.

"I'm sorry." He rubbed his forehead. He'd gotten word about Kalif's new base of operation, and he wanted to go check it out, but then something Zain had said to him today had him thinking about Bobbie.

"What's on your mind?" she asked, as she rubbed his shoulders. Rafi was amazed she could always tell when he was worried about something. He loved her hands on him.

"Just this and that." He reached up and captured her hand. "Come sit down."

She shrugged her shoulders and scooted around the sofa to sit next to him. Rafi took a breath. His insides quivered.

"Bobbie, have you thought about us long term?" Zain had asked him earlier today if he was going to marry Bobbie, and he hadn't been able to stop thinking about it. Bobbie's contract would be up in a few short months, and he didn't want her to leave.

"What do you mean?" She stared at him with those beautiful hazel eyes.

"I mean, I love you and I want a future with you." His declaration was met with silence.

"I'm sorry." Bobbie stood up and began pacing. This wasn't the reaction he was expecting.

"Sweetheart?"

"I never meant ... I didn't want ... " She wrapped her arms around her waist and faced him.

The stark fear on her face had him rising to his feet. "It's okay, sweetheart. We don't have to talk about this now." Had he scared her that much? True, they'd only been together a couple months, but he'd started falling for her that first day on the balcony.

He enfolded her in his arms and cradled her against him. "Nothing has to change." After a few minutes, her body relaxed against his, and her arms went around his waist. "Let's go to bed."

Bobbie lay in bed with Rafi that night and stared at his handsome face. What was she going to do? Well, the simple answer was to break it off with him. But her heart clenched each time she thought about it.

They were both getting in too deep. He'd even said he loved her. She closed her eyes against the pain. He might love her now, but once she told him she was defective inside, that love would disappear. It had before. No. She had to find a way to break it off with him. It was better for both of them.

Rafi deserved better than half a woman. He deserved a woman who could give him everything, but especially children.

Rafi watched Zain in the ring on Friday afternoon with frustration filling him. All week Bobbie had sent Zain down with Hamaz, but she hadn't come down herself. And after dinner, she'd had an excuse each night why she needed to sleep alone.

He'd accepted her excuses. Ever since he'd told her he loved her, Bobbie had been putting a wall between them. He didn't understand why, but right now he had other things to focus on.

Tonight he would ride out to check on Kalif's new setup. He'd leave a note for Khalid telling him what he was doing, but not until he left. He couldn't afford to have

Khalid stopping him. But this was the last time he'd do this. It was getting too risky.

Zain's laughter brought him out of his thoughts. The boy had transformed since the incident in the stables. It was as if the scare had loosened something inside of him. Malik and Catherine were meeting with the advisors to try to figure out a way to adopt Zain, but Rafi had a feeling succession rules weren't going to allow it.

Once Zain was done, Rafi sent him back to the palace with Hamaz, and he rubbed down Ransom. He'd have to leave around dinner time since he would be traveling out further into the desert.

Rafi made sure he had supplies ready and then went up to the palace to shower and change. Tonight he'd get the last piece of the puzzle, and maybe they could be free of Kalif's poppy-growing operation.

Bobbie paced around her room. Rafi hadn't been at dinner. Hassan made a comment that he was probably at the stables, but Bobbie didn't believe it. She was driving him away from his family.

Since his confession, she'd tried keeping her distance from Rafi. On the first day, he'd come after her, trying to coax her down to the stables, but she'd refused. Then that night she'd made up an excuse for them not to sleep together.

By Wednesday he'd stopped asking her why she wouldn't share his bed or come down to the stables with Zain. Dinner last night had been tense, and tonight he hadn't even shown up.

This was never going to work. She needed to leave before her contract ran out. Bobbie flopped on the bed as tears filled her eyes. She didn't want to leave. She wanted to stay. She loved Rafi and Zain and everything.

Bobbie pulled the pillow to her and cried into it. What was she going to do? She was in love with a man, but she couldn't give him children. He was royal and needed to produce heirs. She was screwed. She cried harder into the pillow.

When he and Shadow cleared Bashir City, Rafi breathed a sigh of relief. He stopped to change into his black robe and headdress, and then he and Shadow took off across the sand.

It was close to three in the morning when Rafi finally found where Kalif's men were set up. Too late to get any information, so he retreated to a set of caves he'd found to get some sleep.

He unsaddled Shadow and gave him some food, then made himself a bed from the supplies he'd brought with him. He tried to rest but all he could think about was Bobbie. Had she missed him at dinner tonight? What had her running so scared? Because he'd told her he loved her? Or because he wanted a future with her?

There were more questions than answers. When he got back, he would sit her down and talk to her, because he wasn't willing to let her go. Whatever she was afraid of, they would face it together.

The sun was just breaking the horizon when Rafi dropped off to sleep. It was going to be an uncomfortable day, but he'd survived worse.

Bobbie moped around her room. Rafi wasn't at breakfast, and no one seemed to know where he was. Hamaz told her Rafi had been down at the stables last night. But it was now mid-afternoon, and he still hadn't come up to the palace.

She'd had a sleepless night and come to the conclusion this morning she needed to talk to Rafi. To tell him if he wanted to play, they could, but it couldn't be more than that. She was going to finish out her contract and then go back to Seattle.

The prospect filled her with dread. Maybe she'd see about getting another job overseas. She had enough teaching credentials to find some sort of job. But first she needed to talk to Rafi.

Her determination lasted until she found Hamaz. Everyone insisted the bodyguard walk her down to the stables. She didn't want to air her and Rafi's issues in front of anyone. Maybe Rafi could get him to leave so they could talk.

The sun was high and bright. Bobbie enjoyed the feel of it on her skin. She would miss it if she went back to Seattle. They reached the stable, and she walked in to see Razan.

"Hi, Razan, where's Rafi?" she asked.

"Lady Bobbie," he said. "He's not here. Shadow's stall is empty, so he's probably out for a ride."

"Alone?" Hamaz asked.

"I think so, there are no other horses missing."

Hamaz frowned.

"He does this all the time, Hamaz," Bobbie said.

"Yes, but he's not supposed to." Hamaz's tone told Bobbie he wasn't happy.

"Well, I'll just have to wait until he returns. Razan, please tell Rafi I'm looking for him."

"Of course, Lady Bobbie."

Bobbie and Hamaz walked back to the palace, and Bobbie decided to go to her classroom and set up things for next week while she waited for Rafi to return.

At seven Bobbie walked into the dining room and no Rafi. "Isn't Rafi back yet?" she asked.

"Back?" Hassan asked.

"Razan said he went for a ride, but that was hours ago."

Malik frowned. "That's unusual."

"I'm on it." Khalid strode from the room.

"Rafi will be fine," Catherine said.

"Of course." Malik looked at Bobbie, and she tried to smile, but there was a knot in her stomach. Had she driven Rafi away from his family? One by one they each pushed back from the table and went into the sitting room.

Bobbie paced. This was all her fault. Rafi wanted to be with her and she with him, but not when she couldn't give him children. He was so good with kids. She'd watched him with Zain. It wouldn't be fair to tie him to her.

Even if she told him, Rafi would still want her, but he'd come to resent her, and she couldn't live with that. Damn it, where was he? She turned when Khalid strode into the room, his face grim. She couldn't breathe, and her heart was in her throat.

"Khalid," Malik said.

"Rafi went out into the desert."

"Why?" Catherine asked.

Khalid looked at Bobbie. Her hand fluttered to her throat. He said, "He's been spying on Kalif."

The room erupted, and Bobbie's knees went weak. Spying? Rafi had been taking risks with his life?

Khalid held up his hand. "I only found out recently. Malik, remember I told you about those anonymous notes."

"Yes, they were helping round up some of Kalif's men."

"Rafi was the one leaving them. I caught him one day.

He promised he wouldn't do this without telling me." The paper in his hand crinkled.

"But he did tell you," Sara said, gesturing to the paper.

"No, he didn't tell me before he left. The note just tells me he's going out into the desert to check out Kalif's new operation."

Malik and Hassan both swore. "What do we do?" Malik asked.

"I'll pull together men I trust and we'll try to find Rafi. I'm guessing he left last night since he wasn't at dinner. So he's been gone twenty-four hours."

"Do it." Malik clasped his brother on the shoulder. "Find Rafi."

"I'm going with you," Hassan said.

"No," Khalid said.

"If Rafi's hurt he'll need medical attention."

Bobbie let out a cry as her knees gave way. Rafi hurt?

"Hassan," Sara yelled, and Catherine and Malik rushed to Bobbie's side.

"He said, if, Bobbie," Malik said grasping her arm.

"My fault," she whispered. She couldn't breathe.

"No, it isn't." Catherine and Malik helped her to the sofa.

But it was her fault. If she hadn't broken off with him, would he have gone out? Probably not; he would have been safe in her bed. Oh, dear Lord. She covered her face with her hands as tears filled her eyes.

"Go," Catherine said.

"I'll be in my office," Malik said. "Stay here. Samir and Najah will be right outside the door." The sound of footsteps reached Bobbie's ears and then the click of a door closing.

The sofa dipped on both sides of Bobbie, and then arms went around her shoulders. "It will be okay," Sara's soft voice floated over her.

"Sara's right. They'll find Rafi," Catherine said.

Bobbie shook her head. "This is all my fault." What was she going to do? Rafi had to be okay. Every nerve in her body screamed at her to do something, but what? Yes, she could go riding with the men, but she'd be more of a hindrance than a help.

"Honey, you are not to blame," Catherine said, rubbing her back.

"But I am." Bobbie lifted her head from her hands. "He told me he loved me, and I pushed him away."

"You did?" Sara said, disbelief in her voice.

"Why would you do that, Bobbie? You love him," Catherine said.

"I do, but ... " Could she reveal her problem? What did it matter? She'd driven Rafi away. She closed her eyes and prayed for his safe return. When she opened them, both Sara and Catherine were staring at her. "I'm broken," she whispered.

"Oh, honey, we all are," Catherine said, giving her a hug.

Bobbie shook her head. "Not like me."

"What do you mean?" Sara asked.

"I'm unable to have children." The words spilled out of her along with tears. She'd been fooling herself to ever think she and Rafi could have a relationship. Play together, yes. Sex, yes. But an actual relationship? No.

"Oh, Bobbie," whispered Catherine. Both women tightened their arms around her.

"He doesn't know, I can't tell him. He'll only say it doesn't matter, but it does." Her voice warbled as she talked. "He's second in line, he needs children of his own."

"Here." A handful of tissues were thrust into her hands.

Bobbie took a deep breath and tried to pull herself together. She never fell apart like this, not since her father had died. But her heart hurt, and she was so worried for Rafi. She mopped up her tears and blew her nose.

"Better?" asked Catherine.

"I think so."

"Good; now, who said you can't have children?" Sara asked.

"Short version, when I first started getting my cycle, I'd have terrible cramps and then heavy periods. Then irregular cycles. My doctor assumed it was being young and because I was athletic with horses. But it never got better. It continued until I was in my early twenties, when my cycle disappeared totally. I was diagnosed with a type of PCOS."

Sara nodded. "I'm sorry."

"What is PCOS?" Catherine asked.

"Basically a hormonal imbalance that prevents normal ovulation," Sara said.

"So there's no chance?" Catherine asked.

"Not for me."

"I don't understand. There are treatments for PCOS," Sara said.

"There are, but nothing has worked on me. The doctor isn't sure why. When I was twenty-four, they found cysts growing at an alarming rate. They were cancerous. So I had surgery."

"Hysterectomy," Sara whispered.

Bobbie nodded.

"Oh, shit, I'm sorry." Catherine squeezed her hand.

Bobbie's heart clenched. There, she'd said it. She glanced at her watch. Thirty minutes. How could it be only thirty minutes had passed? "I can't stand this."

"We're here for you," Sara said. "And what you said about driving Rafi away is untrue. He's always been the dark horse of the family. He may act all flirty and charming, but I've always known there was something else lurking below the surface."

"Since we're stuck here for a while, why don't I call down to the kitchen for some ice cream and cookies? If there was ever a time for comfort food, this is it," Catherine said, standing.

"Actually, that sounds good," Bobbie said, and it did.

Maybe she could drown her worries in ice cream. That is, if the wait didn't kill her.

Rafi crept closer to the row of tents. He needed to be careful ... if he got caught ... No, he wouldn't think like that. This was his last job. Once he was done with this he was hanging up his spying gig. He had more important things in his life. Bobbie.

Spending the day in the cave had given him a lot of time to think. She was pushing him away for some reason. Damn it, he'd seen the love in her eyes after they'd made love.

He wasn't going to let her go so easily. He loved her, and he wanted her for his wife. They could overcome any problem. Light flared inside the tent in front of him. Rafi settled down to listen.

Bobbie woke with a start and then let out a groan. She'd fallen asleep on the sofa last night, and now her neck was stiff. She sat up to see Catherine and Sara sitting across from her.

Her heart sank. She'd hoped Rafi would come home in the middle of the night. "No sign of him?" Her voice was still husky with sleep. Catherine and Sara looked at each other. "Tell me."

"Shadow came back riderless early this morning," Catherine said.

Bobbie froze. Riderless? "Oh, dear Lord," Bobbie whispered. Anything could have happened to Rafi. Shadow wasn't one to bolt. "Do they ... " She swallowed hard. "Do they have any clues what happened?"

"No," Sara said.

This wasn't good; no, it wasn't. Bobbie was tired of sitting here waiting. She stood and moved to the door.

"Where are you going?" Catherine asked.

"The stables, I might be able to tell something from Shadow." She pulled open the door to be brought up short by Samir and Najah. "Out of my way."

"Lady Bobbie," Samir started.

"No. You can come with me or get Hamaz, but I'm going to the stables, and no one is stopping me." She knew they were under orders to keep the women safe, but damn if she'd sit here if she could help.

Bobbie strode past the two men, only to see Hamaz standing by the door that led out toward the stables. "I will accompany you, my lady."

She nodded and together they went down to the stables. The mood there wasn't much better than at the house. The stable hands were quiet. She went to Shadow's stall and found the horse pacing around.

"It's okay, Shadow," she whispered. The black head turned in her direction, and he came to the stable door.

Bobbie stroked his neck, and Shadow whinnied. "I know, boy. What happened out there?"

She opened the stall and stepped inside. Shadow looked good. He'd been rubbed down and brushed. He brushed his head against her arm.

"I cleaned him up, Lady Bobbie," Razan, the stable hand, said.

"Thank you, Razan. How did Shadow look when he came in?" she asked.

"Tired and hungry, but otherwise unhurt."

"Was the saddle still on?"

"Yes."

Bobbie fought to keep the tears at bay. That meant Rafi had either been on Shadow or Shadow had run off. She was going with the former. "Was there anything you found on the horse that maybe could tell us where Rafi is?"

"No, Lady Bobbie. I'm sorry."

"It's okay, Razan." Bobbie stroked Shadow a few more times before exiting the stall. "Razan, would you saddle Gypsy for me?"

"I can't allow that, Bobbie."

She turned to see Malik standing inside the stable doors, every inch the king.

"Excuse me," Razan said, leaving the stable.

"Malik, I need to do something." Didn't he understand? Rafi was out there alone and possibly hurt. She needed to get to him. She needed to tell him she was sorry and how much she loved him.

"I know you want to." Malik strode over to her and took her by the shoulders. "I want to help too, but we can't. You going out on Gypsy alone isn't the way."

"I can ride." She raised her chin.

"I'm aware of that, but you don't even know where to look."

"But ... " Tears filled her eyes.

"I know." He pulled her into his arms, giving her comfort. "Khalid and his security forces are out there. They will find him."

"How can you be so sure?" She tried to push back her fears and tears.

"Because I know my brothers. They are not going to give up, and Rafi is smart, he'll find a way home."

"But Shadow came back alone."

"True, but we don't know why. Razan said the horse had run a long way, as if he'd been sent away. There were no injuries to Shadow, nothing to indicate any type of harm."

"True." Bobbie forced herself away from Malik's comfort. She needed to learn to stand on her own two feet like she had after her father died. *Don't think that way. Rafi will be fine.*

"Come back to the house. Breakfast is waiting." He took her by the elbow and guided her from the stables.

"I'm not hungry." The bright sunshine mocked her.

Lord, she hoped Rafi was okay. Because she would never forgive herself if he was hurt because of her. Maybe she should have told him. She could still have insisted they not marry, but at least he'd understand why, and maybe he wouldn't have gone out into the desert.

"You need to eat. None of us ate last night." Malik nodded to Hamaz, who followed behind them.

"You're not going to allow me to find Rafi, are you?" Bobbie looked up at Malik.

"No. Food … and we'll go from there."

Bobbie shook her head. Stubborn male. Hell, all the al-Hakim men were. That made her brighten a little bit. Rafi was stubborn too, and he'd fight to get back home. He had to.

Rafi stared at the beautiful yellow and orange sunset against the clear blue sky. Time to start walking. His family was going to be in an uproar, but it couldn't be helped.

He had to travel the desert at night; during the day he wouldn't last long. Night had its own hazards, but he'd grown up here. He could avoid them.

Hell, he was damn lucky to be alive. After hearing the information he needed, he had been sneaking away when one of the men had decided to take a leak and saw him. While the two had tussled, Rafi had taken him down and then taken off.

He'd known his time was short, so he sent Shadow off, knowing the horse would make his way back to the stables while Rafi took off in another direction. His plan had worked. While Kalif's men had searched the cave where he'd been hiding and then pursued the hoof-prints across the desert, he'd taken off toward the east and found another set of caves.

Rafi had bunked down there for the night, staying awake just in case he had to fight his way out. But Kalif's men had never found him. He'd heard their muffled voices, but they'd stayed away from the cave. He'd been damn lucky.

By the time nightfall had arrived, there was no one around, and he thanked his lucky stars. Now he put one foot in front of the other. It was a long way back to the palace, but he knew his brothers.

When Shadow returned without him, they would start looking for him. Thank goodness he'd left that note on Khalid's desk letting him know the general direction he was going. Maybe they would meet halfway. At least he had a few provisions, some protein bars and water.

When night started giving way to day, Rafi found shelter at an old oasis he'd passed. He was probably about a quarter of the way home. At least now he was far enough away it was doubtful Kalif's men would be looking for him.

He sank down next to the water, splashed it on his face, and wet his headdress before wrapping it back around his head. It wasn't going to be a comfortable day, but he'd survive.

As the sun began to rise in the sky, he thought about Bobbie. His sweet, sexy woman. When he got back they were going to sit down and talk, because whatever she was hiding, he wanted to know what it was.

He'd thought a lot yesterday hiding in the cave. He wasn't ready to let Bobbie go. These few days apart had made his heart ache. He wanted her in his life, no matter what. The family had survived bigger issues than she knew. His brothers would back him up, and so would Catherine and Sara.

Rafi closed his eyes and tried to rest. He had another long day and night in front of him.

The sound of horses made Rafi stop before he climbed over the next hill. He lay down on his stomach and inched his way up until he could see over the rise. His breath rushed out of him as he stood up. Rafi waved his arms at the men on horses. It was his brother and his security team.

"It's about time," he said, as Khalid dismounted.

Khalid didn't say a word, just enveloped Rafi in a tight hug. "Thank goodness we found you." Khalid's voice was husky.

"I'm fine, brother." Rafi hugged his brother back.

"When Shadow came back without you ... " Khalid pushed him to arm's length and shook his head. "You're done with spying."

Rafi opened his mouth. "Yes, he is," Hassan said walking up to the pair. The brothers embraced. "Are you hurt anywhere?"

"I'm fine. A little hungry and thirsty, but that's it," Rafi said.

"I'll accept that for now, but once we get back I want to give you a quick physical to make sure," Hassan said.

"I didn't bring Shadow with us, but another horse. Can you ride?" Khalid asked.

"Yes. How mad is Malik?"

"He wasn't happy, but I think you'd better worry more about Bobbie, Catherine, and Sara," Hassan said, as they mounted their horses.

"Is Bobbie okay?" He hated the fact he had worried her, but it had been unavoidable.

"She was worried when we left. Since then I don't know. I didn't want to risk using the satellite phone just in case we needed it later," Khalid said.

Rafi nodded. "Let's get back so I can calm everyone down."

Khalid nodded, Rafi mounted the horse, and they all took off.

Bobbie blinked, trying to clear the grit out of her eyes. Barely sleeping for two days will do that to you. She'd eaten a little to stop Catherine and Sara from badgering her. But they were ganging up on her to get some sleep.

She needed some time alone, so she had Hamaz walk her to the stables. Dawn would be here soon, another dawn without Rafi. Bobbie stroked Shadow's head when he stuck it out the stall door.

"I know, Shadow. I miss him too," she whispered.

The thundering of horses made her stiffen. Without thought, she ran to the stable doors. "Lady Bobbie, please hide yourself," he said.

"Hamaz, there's so much security I'm sure not even an ant could get onto the palace grounds without being caught. It has to be Khalid and Hassan." She kept her eyes on the path leading up to the stables.

Within a couple of minutes, horses came trotting up the path. Bobbie blinked several times. Rafi. Her knees went weak as he pulled the horse to a stop and dismounted. She didn't even hesitate; she ran and threw herself into his arms.

"You're okay." Tears spilled down her cheeks in relief and in anger. She leaned back. "Don't ever do that to me again." She punctuated her words by hitting him in the chest.

"I'm sorry, sweetheart." He captured her fists in his hands and kissed each one in turn. "I never meant to scare anyone."

"What happened?" she asked.

"Why don't we go up to the house, and I can explain to everyone at once," he said.

Bobbie nodded and started to disentangle herself from Rafi, but he slipped his arm around her waist and pulled her to his side.

"I'm not letting you get away, now or ever," he whispered.

Her heart pounded, and she wanted to believe his words. She'd done a lot of thinking while he was missing. She still couldn't stay with him, not when she couldn't have children, but she'd take the time she had with him until her contract was over. Her heart was already broken, so what were a few more dents?

Upon his arrival in the family room, Sara and Catherine welcomed him back with hugs. Malik too, then Malik took Rafi to task about doing something so dangerous. Bobbie hid a smile; they were happy to see Rafi, and yet they weren't letting him get away with scaring them. Food and drink were brought in. Rafi kept her by his side when they sat down.

"So what happened?" Malik asked.

Rafi cleared his throat. "One of Kalif's men saw me spying. I sent Shadow home and hid in the caves until the next night."

"You must have been pretty far out if it took over two nights for anyone to find you," Sara said.

Bobbie concentrated on her food. If she thought about

what Rafi had done, she'd lose all control of her emotions. She was barely holding on as it was.

"Yeah, but I have the location of Kalif's new base of operation. It was worth it."

"Like hell," Malik commented and all eyes turned to him. Bobbie wanted to cheer. "Nothing is worth your life, Rafi. Not now, not ever."

Silence descended. Khalid stood. "Malik is right." Khalid placed a hand on Rafi's shoulder and his other hand on hers. "You have someone special now. You must take care of yourself."

"Enough," Catherine said. "I'm glad Rafi is home and safe. Let's eat and then you men can talk strategy and stuff."

Bobbie let out a little laugh. Leave it to Catherine to put the men in their places. Rafi slipped his arm over Bobbie's shoulders and gave her a squeeze. "Okay?" he asked.

"I'll be fine." But would she?

By the time they'd finished eating it was midmorning, and everyone was yawning. Malik and Catherine retired first. Khalid went to give the men who had ridden with them in the desert some time off and make sure the rest of the security staff was covered.

Hassan insisted on checking Rafi out. They disappeared for about twenty minutes before coming back and Hassan telling Bobbie Rafi was fine. Then Hassan picked up Sara, who'd fallen asleep on the sofa, and carried her to their room.

She stared at Rafi as he held out his hand to her. "Let's go get some sleep, my love."

Unable to stop herself, Bobbie put her hand in his and allowed him to lead her up to his bedroom. She was so tired. Rafi undressed her and put her on the bed before he stripped and joined her.

"Sleep, my love," he said, gathering her into his arms. "I'll be here when you wake up."

"You'd better be."

Bobbie woke the next morning in the arms of the man she loved. She wasn't going to hide it from herself anymore. She loved Rafi. But they didn't have a future together, not really.

"Good morning, my love," Rafi said, his lips brushing the top of her head.

She tilted her head up from where it rested on his chest to see his dark eyes on her. "Morning." She closed her eyes, enjoying the feel of his heart beating beneath her ear. So many things could have gone wrong while he was out in the desert.

"I'm all right," he said, as if knowing what she was thinking.

"Now," she whispered. "I don't know what I would

have done if something had happened to you." Bobbie wanted to yell at him, but she couldn't, not when he was holding her in his arms.

"I won't put myself in that position again," he said.

"You'd better not." Bobbie leaned up on her elbow. "My heart couldn't take it."

Rafi stared at her. "I meant what I said before, Bobbie. I love you and I want a life with you."

Her heart sank, and she closed her eyes. What she wouldn't give to stay with Rafi. But it couldn't be. Not when she couldn't bear him a child or two. "I'm sorry, Rafi," she whispered.

"I know you love me." Warm fingers caressed her cheek.

Bobbie opened her eyes. "I do." She wasn't going to lie to him, not after all they'd been through.

"Then what is the problem, sweetheart? Is it because I'm royal?"

"Yes, and no." When he frowned, she continued, "I don't mind your being royal, but it's your place in the royal life that might create a problem."

"Explain your thinking to me."

Bobbie maneuvered herself into a sitting position. "You're the second son."

"Yes." He stared at her.

"And it means your children could one day inherit the throne."

"Is that what you're worried about?" He sat up. "Baby,

once Malik and Catherine start having children, we'll be way down the line. Our succession rules are not very complicated."

"But that's just it, there are succession rules."

"There are for most royal families." He wiggled his nose. "Is it the press attention that bothers you?"

"A bit, but not that much."

"Then what, sweetheart? I can't help you get over the fear if you don't tell me what it is."

"It's not a fear, but reality." She took a deep breath. "I can't have children."

Rafi flinched, and Bobbie's heart sank. Yes, children were important to him.

"How do you know?" he asked softly, before covering her trembling hand with his.

"I had to have a hysterectomy a couple of years ago."

"So there is nothing that can be done?"

She shook her head. "This is why we can't stay together." Bobbie lowered her gaze to her lap.

"Bobbie, look at me." He waited until she lifted her head. "I love you. Your ability to have children or not doesn't affect my love."

"Rafi, don't." Tears filled her eyes and spilled down her cheeks.

"I mean it." He wiped the tears away with his thumb, but more kept coming. "Please don't cry. We can figure this out."

"But how? You're expected to have heirs."

"True, but I will probably never become king." He pulled the sheet up and dried her tears.

"But there's a chance," she said. "I can't deny you that chance or the chance for your children to rule."

"Sweetheart," he said, and put his arms around her and pulled her into his embrace. "We'll figure this out."

"How? It's not like it's something that can be ignored or cleared up. I'm broken, Rafi."

His head snapped up and his eyes blazed. "You are not broken." His tone was hard and low. "You are the woman I love." He took a deep breath. "Let's get dressed and go discuss this with the family. Maybe they'll have some ideas."

Bobbie nodded. Catherine and Sara already knew, and if she and Rafi were going to have any chance at a relationship, the rest of his family needed to know as well.

The entire family sat around the dining room table, and all eyes were on Bobbie. She squirmed in her chair, but she couldn't blame them. The news Rafi had just imparted was shocking.

"Is this why you broke it off with Rafi?" Malik asked.

"Yes," she whispered. "I understand he needs to have children of his own."

Rafi took her hand in his. "Children aren't everything," he told her.

"Rafi is right." Hassan said. "Malik?"

"I believe there are provisions in the records. I'll have to pull them out and see." Malik steepled his fingers and stared at Rafi and her. "But no matter what they say, Bobbie, rules can be changed."

Bobbie swallowed. "I want to be fair to Rafi."

"Baby, between my brothers and their wives, I suspect there is going to be a house full of nieces and nephews to love and spoil."

"And there's always adoption," Catherine said.

"One step at a time, my love," Malik said. "Let me see what the rules say now, and we'll go from there."

"Of course." Catherine leaned over and gave him a kiss. "I know you'll find a solution."

The solution took time to find, but Malik, Hassan, and Rafi finally found it in the old records after three days of searching.

Bobbie was sitting in the garden when Rafi found her. The smile on his face made hope grow in her heart.

"Well?" she asked.

"There is a provision. Actually one that will solve a couple of problems."

"Tell me."

Rafi sat down next to her and faced her. He took her hands in his. "First off, I want you to know I've already made my decision."

"We should discuss it before you make any decision." She frowned at him.

"I just spent the last four hours discussing it with my brothers. They agree with me, and it is my choice."

She nodded, but another matter was pressing on her mind. "What about Kalif?" She didn't know if she could handle his spying.

"Not to worry. I've been given orders by my King. No more spying." He grinned at her. "Khalid and his security force will take care of him and the poppy fields."

"All right. Tell me what you found."

"We found an old law that allows me to abdicate out of being in the line of succession."

Bobbie shook her head. "No, Rafi, you can't. You can't give it up. I won't let you."

"Which is why it's already done." He held up his hand when she went to speak. "I was aware you would object, but being king was never part of my makeup."

"But your family." She couldn't believe he'd done this without discussing it with her first.

"They understand, and remember what I said, this solves more than one problem."

"What's the other problem?"

"Zain."

"What does any of this have to do with Zain?" She could barely wrap her head around what he'd done.

"Catherine wanted to adopt Zain, but they can't because of the succession."

"Right, I remember them talking about that. I thought they were basically going to make Zain their ward."

"There were roadblocks, but by my giving up any rights to the throne, we can adopt Zain."

"What?" Bobbie's eyes grew wide.

"Think of it, Bobbie. We marry and adopt Zain. We have our family, and later we can adopt more kids."

"Rafi, are you sure this is what you want? You're giving up so much."

"I'm giving up all the pressure of worrying about being king, that's all. I still have my family, and soon I'll have you and Zain to add to it."

"Rafi, I don't know what to say."

"Say yes." Rafi stood then knelt down and took her hand in his. "Will you marry me?"

"Yes."

Rafi let out a yell then scooped her into his arms. Within a minute they were surrounded by the guards, and Bobbie couldn't help but laugh.

ACKNOWLEDGMENTS

To my critique group who always supports me

ABOUT THE AUTHOR

Marie Tuhart lives in the beautiful Pacific Northwest with her muse, Penny, a four-pound toy poodle. Marie loves to read and write. When she's not writing, she spends time with family, traveling and enjoying life.

Marie is a multi-published author with The Wild Rose Press, Trifecta Publishing House and does some self-publishing. To be alerted on new releases on Amazon or Book Bub, you can join Marie's newsletter where she gives her group advance information on her books, runs contests and does giveaways just for newsletter readers. Marie can also be found on Pinterest, Twitter, and Facebook.